Check Engine and
Other Stories

by

Jennifer Companik

Check Engine and Other Stories

ISBN-13: 978-1-7345158-9-3

Cover image: "Dive" by Reinier Lensink

Printed in the U.S.A.

For more titles and inquiries, please visit:

www.thirtywestph.com

Table of Contents

Madre me ha prevenido, me previene: Cuídate del lobo, mi tierna niñita candida, inocente, frágil, vestidita de rojo.

¿Por qué me mandó al bosque, entonces? ¿Por qué es inevitable el camino que conduce a la abuela?

~

Mother has warned me, she warns: Beware of the wolf, my tender little naïf, my innocent, fragile, little girl dressed in red.

Why send me into the forest, then? Why is the path that leads to grandmother so inevitable?

—Luisa Valenzuela, from, "If This Is Life, I'm Little Red Riding Hood".
Translated from the Spanish by Jennifer Companik.

Check Engine and Other Stories

The Pet Store

I seldom visited pet stores in my regular, pre-parenthood, adult life. Having never owned a real pet like a dog or cat or even a parrot, I always felt pet store employees could tell from my bearing and scent that I didn't belong there, plus I'd stopped keeping pets in the sixth grade. Oh, once in a while, when I was lonely because Bill had to work late, I'd window shop and wander into the pet store in the mall to stare at the puppies—sometimes asking to hold whichever one looked the softest, sometimes curling up to the idea of buying one—but stopping short when I remembered my childhood experiences at keeping small creatures alive, always deciding in the last minute to spare them.

***

When I was nine, I saved six months' allowance to purchase an aquarium. Then, I oversaw the deaths of twelve fish and one seahorse in three months—through overfeeding, underfeeding, incorrect Ph balance in the water, tank malfunction, mixing of aggressive and non-aggressive fish in the tank, accidental poisoning, intentional poisoning by my little sister Marchie, and unexplained quietus.

I gave up on pet ownership for a year after that.

Then I bought a hamster.

I fared no better with hamsters. They averaged a couple of months apiece. Marchie started calling me the "Grim Reaper of Animals." After the second hamster died, I raised plants.

Despite all this, yesterday I found myself in this pet store killing time with my four-year-old son, Teddy, before my doctor's appointment. Teddy loved it so much, I told him we'd come back today.

This particular pet store lacks the fetid, desperate-animal smell I associate with such places. The plastic chew toys off-gas less in this store than in others—or maybe the air is fresher because the backdoor is open, allowing an occasional cool breeze inside. The store smells mostly of cedar mingled with a hamster-piss odor I recognize from my childhood.

Teddy sits cross-legged on the floor in front of the puppy display. The puppies live one or two to a box in what looks like a three-story apartment building set against the back wall of the store. Teddy watches as the two puppies in the ground floor 'apartment' scrap over a set of plastic keys. The bigger puppy pins its suitemate—the smaller dog's ear between the larger one's teeth.

"No biting!" Teddy shouts at the bigger puppy, then, tapping compassionately on the glass, "Don't worry; it will heal!" to the smaller one.

Teddy, an only child, really talks like that.

I shift from one foot to the other in moderate pain. The prescription pain pills made me too groggy to function, so I took acetaminophen instead which has only slightly blunted the pain. I'm waiting for Teddy to get bored, but he doesn't, so I watch the animals. On the top floor of the puppy apartment building is a fluffy Maltese with an air about her like that of a confused, elderly woman. Unlike the beagle and the pug two floors down, the Maltese stare out at the pet store patrons. Or maybe she sees her reflection—she doesn't appear to notice us. She's on sale. I wonder if she senses that she's two-hundred dollars cheaper today than she was yesterday. I wonder if it troubles her.

My mother says life is troubles punctuated by smiles. For dogs, maybe instead of smiles, you could say 'tail waggings.' I'm not sure. I think about how much heartbreak people save dogs by having them fixed.

Only nothing is ever fixed.

***

I wasn't supposed to get pregnant. I'd hemorrhaged after giving birth to Teddy, and the infection following the surgery it took to stop the bleeding caused scar tissue to build in my uterus. Asherman's Syndrome, they called it. So much scar tissue, they explained, it was 'extremely unlikely' I'd conceive again without more surgery. I was only twenty-four years old and in no hurry to repeat the agony I went through having Teddy, so Bill and I agreed I should not undergo surgery to *maybe* regain my fertility. Yet I got happy when I found out I was pregnant. It felt like a reversal of fate: a miracle—Teddy would have a brother or sister after all.

My OBGYN warned me not to get my hopes up, but my hopes climbed a little higher each day. If I could get pregnant against the odds, I could carry to term against the odds. He advised me to 'take it easy.' I haven't so much as lifted Teddy in a month.

"I'm ready to go," I say to Teddy, feeling shaky, remembering I am supposed to avoid standing until this is over, worried for a second about violating doctors' orders, then falling hard on the thought that following doctors' orders guarantees nothing.

Teddy looks up at me, his eyes full of puppies. "Five more minutes, Mommy. Please?"

"Okay, Baby."

Five more minutes won't kill me. And if the bleeding gets

worse, the hospital is across the street.

I put my hand over my womb. The cramping has subsided a little. Dr. Haversoll said the D&C could wait a few days until Bill gets back from his meeting in China, that it's not urgent, that the pregnancy wasn't far enough along for the procedure to be urgent.

I haven't told Bill.

If I think about this again, I'll cry. Teddy will hug me and ask me if I'm okay and ask me if it will heal and offer to kiss the spot that hurts, and I'll cry harder. When Bill comes home, I can cry privately—I use this thought like cotton to soak up the tears in my head.

I study the dogs, grinding my teeth in pain. Today I must be strong. Tomorrow I can cry.

There are two dogs—a Jack Russell and a collie—in the apartment between the old-lady dog and the scrappers; they are easy to overlook. They've had their backs to the window and spent the last ten minutes cuddling in their nook, half-asleep, the way Bill and I do after a long day when he's not in a meeting in China. A lady walks up with her pre-teen daughters. She wants to buy the Jack Russell. The collie raises her head as a store employee removes her companion, then she sits up and stares at the door through which he's been removed. She stays that way as if taxidermized.

She's still sitting up, back to the window, staring at the door like that when Teddy bounces up and tugs on my skirt.

"Mommy," he says. "Can I have a puppy?"

"Which one do you think you want?" I say, not wanting to say no right away, trying to call up the strength to deal with the tantrum he'll throw when I say no.

He points at the collie. "That one."

"Why that one?" I ask, surprised, hoping he can't tell how close I am to tears.

Teddy looks at me with his serious eyes—eyes just like Bill's but set in an expression that otherwise reflects a smaller, cuter, brown-eyed version of my father. Yes, Teddy reminds me of dad—did from the day he was born. Bill saw it, too—it was Bill who suggested we name Teddy after my stalwart, tender father.

Teddy. How I love his soft, sticky face; his watermelon-and-corn-chips smell; the gentleness with which he kisses my cheek to wake me each morning, laughing at my sleepiness and saying, "The sun is up!" For a moment, I forget the pain in my lower abdomen and smile at my son.

He wiggles his doughty little hand into mine.

"That one looks sad," he says, pointing at the collie with his free hand. "I want to make her happy."

Check Engine

How long had her check engine light been on? Gwen could not recall.

"Mommy!"

"Yes, Baby?"

"Mommy! Mommy! Mommy!"

"What is it, Son?"

"Are you listening?"

No. She hadn't been listening. Between the ice on the road, the trucker following too closely behind her, the pain in her stomach, and the check engine light—no, she had not heard anything Raleigh said. Plus, Raleigh said more words in one hour than a sportscaster said during a World Cup soccer match. Raleigh had Attention-Deficit/Hyperactivity Disorder (ADHD), and while he took medication to control his symptoms, Ritalin did nothing to dam her son's endless surge of words.

"You never listen to me!"

Not true—but he was, as Gwen's psychiatrist would say, "expressing a feeling, not a fact."

"I'm sorry, Baby. I don't feel well, and it's tough driving in the snow." She made eye contact in the rear-view mirror. "What were you saying?"

Raleigh sobbed. "I forgot."

"Let me know when you remember."

Raleigh cried the biggest tears of anyone Gwen had ever seen cry. Tears, it seemed, the size of bottle caps. On a day when her stomach didn't feel like she'd swallowed a block of knives, Gwen might've worried that, at nine, Raleigh was too old to cry as often as he did. But Gwen couldn't sense much beyond her pain—there were the survival challenges of black ice on the roadway, the tailgating trucker, and now, the check engine light. Raleigh's sobs blurred to background noise as they had for years.

Ten miles. Ten miles to go until they reached the doctor's office.

The only reason Raleigh was along for this was that school was out for Presidents' Day. Gwen's doctor had urged her to come to the office today to discuss the treatment of her newly diagnosed syndrome which boiled down to ulcers. Gwen was thirty-three years old and had ulcers. The first time she walked into the gastroenterologist's waiting room, she looked around and walked out thinking, "I'm thirty-seven years early for this appointment." She'd sat in her parked car for an hour, convincing herself she was just stressed out and would be totally fine without going to see an old-people doctor. Then she shat blood for a week straight. She rescheduled the appointment. The doctor performed tests: CT scans, an MRI, x-rays, x-rays with contrast, blood tests, fasting blood tests, a colonoscopy. By the end of the two months of testing, Gwen felt exhausted and depressed despite the 20 milligrams of Lexapro she took each day. "A voodoo doll," she'd told her psychiatrist. "I feel like an angry person's voodoo doll."

The tests showed Gwen suffered from Irritable Bowel Syndrome. It sounded like a made-up disease to Gwen—something her Doctor Barbie would've told her Patient Barbie she had when she was ten. Her ten-year-old self read textbooks for fun and watched *Oprah*, so while she might not have known what 'bowel' or 'syndrome' meant exactly, that would have been half the fun; and Patient Barbie would've gone into amusing hysterics and asked the question she always asked Doctor Barbie after a diagnosis: "Am I going to die?!" Sometimes Doctor Barbie gave Patient Barbie 'pills' (Tic Tacs) and told her she'd be fine. Other times Doctor Barbie shook her head somberly and told her there was no cure and that she would just have to try to die bravely.

"We'll be there in fifteen minutes."

"Did you know honey never goes bad?" Raleigh asked.

"No, I didn't know that."

"Archeologists found some in King Tut's tomb and ate it. It was seven thousand years old, and nothing happened to the archeologists. They were fine. Can you believe that?"

At least Raleigh's tear storms had shortened over the years. As a baby, he'd cried seven hours a day, refusing to nurse, then stayed awake all night, clamped to her chest, a hungry marsupial. Matt had badgered Gwen to give up breastfeeding. She didn't. She wouldn't. Breastfeeding was the only time Gwen felt happy as a mother, but the lack of rest broke her. After two months of no sleep, Gwen felt so close to smothering Raleigh in his crib that she checked herself into the hospital. No one understood. Matt had visited her during the five days she spent in the psych ward, staring at his lap, recoiling from her touch, and talking about how Raleigh loved drinking formula from a bottle. Gwen kept her thoughts about smothering Matt in his bed to herself, as those thoughts seemed more normal. What woman didn't, at some point, fantasize about killing her husband?

"A group of frogs is called a knot."

"That's excellent, Son. You know I love collective nouns."

Besides, Gwen was over feeling afraid of her violent thoughts by then. Her doctor in the psych ward did a good job convincing her of the profound difference between thought and action.

Gwen knew she needed certain things in life—things like unbroken sleep, regular meals, sexual comfort, and adult conversation—things incompatible with mothering a child of Raleigh's temperament. She'd spent nine years feeling like a brass-buttoned soldier losing against a guerilla force.

If it wasn't the boy, it was the man.

Matt opposed all her efforts to teach Raleigh to self-soothe. Gwen studied books on how to get babies to sleep, but any time she tried to let Raleigh cry it out, or even if she followed the (absurdly specific) time intervals for picking him up when he fussed at night, Matt would have not one but *two* baby monitors (one with a video camera trained at an irate Raleigh howling in his crib) screeching at her. He also wouldn't follow the books' instructions. Or Gwen's. Even if Raleigh fell asleep in his crib by mistake, Matt would set him next to Gwen in their bed before he left for work in the morning. He did this even when she explained that this meant that three or four times a week she woke up in a puddle of piss. Or shit. Matt would then look at her like she lacked maternal feeling. If Gwen took a nap on the weekend, Matt would feed Raleigh a bottle instead of calling her to nurse him, even after she explained that his doing so caused her physical pain when her breasts filled expectantly with milk without a hungry baby to empty them. "You can always pump," Matt said. Anytime he said that Gwen imagined fastening a powerful suction pump to Matt's penis and telling him to use *that* anytime he felt engorged *there*—not that Matt ever approached her for sex.

When, at age four, Raleigh finally slept through the night, Gwen dreamed about having another child—a girl, maybe; maybe adopted—the second time around had to be easier, right?

Her ideal family had always included two children. But Matt didn't want more kids; had had a vasectomy without consulting her and didn't want to adopt. Plus, Gwen's fantasies about Matt had not grown kinder in the four years since they'd had Raleigh, so she smothered her dream instead.

The trucker finally passed her. Her doctor's office was three miles away. What should she do about the check engine light? Call Matt? Drag Raleigh to the car dealership? Wait until tomorrow? She couldn't miss this appointment. She hated not knowing what to do.

Matt, the lead engineer at an auto factory, knew about cars. He could put one together if you handed him the parts and a bucket of tools. Gwen possessed analogous knowledge of poetry—practical whenever she haggled over the price of a sestina. Any time she walked into a car repair shop, they smelled her lack of car savvy and padded her bill. If she called Matt first and the problem was too urgent for him to fix in his scant spare time (and it often was) he could arm her with an idea of what might be wrong and what the job should cost. She could then at least negotiate with her captors.

If only her ulcers wouldn't bleed.

She pulled into the doctor's office parking lot.

"Bring your book, Baby. And your pencil and drawing paper. I don't know how long that'll take, but you can't come into the examining room with me, and I don't want you to be bored."

"Okay, Mommy," he said, then went on: "But did you know that a group of dolphins is called a pod? And a group of leopards is called a leap? And a group of hippopotamuses is called a bloat?" He gathered his things into the backpack on the seat beside him while he chattered. The backpack was their Everything Bag: snacks, amusements, medication, first aid.

Gwen knew she was not a perfect mother, but she planned well.

Before Raleigh started on Ritalin, getting him to take his Everything Bag had sparked conflagrations of protest. The "Okay, Mommy" with compliance was new and infinitely better than having the bag (or its contents) hurled at her which was what used to happen, privately and publicly. Gwen felt so accustomed to the judging stares of strangers—and, if she let herself think about it, friends—she nearly kissed the sensibly shod feet of the first person who said to her: "What a well-behaved young man you have there." Six months ago, they'd been standing in a long grocery-checkout line, Raleigh reciting "Daddy Fell into the Pond" by Alfred Noyes; the compliment came from a smiling, white-haired woman. Raleigh had just turned nine. In nine years, no one had remarked kindly on his conduct, the subtext of the silence always "What a terrible mother you must be to have such a misbehaved child."

Gwen set Raleigh up in a corner of the waiting room and checked in with the receptionist. She watched her son read while the receptionist took her copayment. *He can read now*, she thought with relief.

It had taken him much longer than his peers to learn. His ADHD made it hard for him to focus and hold still—two things critical to learning how to read. When, at the end of third grade, they threatened to hold him back because his standardized reading scores showed he read at a first-grade level, Gwen moved him to a Montessori school. Matt did not want Raleigh in some "hippie private school," but this time Gwen fought to win. Gwen's general philosophy on conflict with Matt was that, since he always fought (and shouted, and called names, and woke her in the middle of the night when she was trying to sleep, or barged in on her when she was in the bathroom trying to use the toilet) to win any argument, she would fight to remain on good terms with Matt, even if that meant "losing" most of the time—she believed there was often greater wisdom in surrender than in battle.

But she would not let some test ruin Raleigh's experience of learning. This was not a fight about the affair she had when Raleigh was two—for which Matt had never forgiven her—or a fight about her wanting a shred of privacy back now that seven years had passed. Gwen had chosen to stay married to Matt. Had she known his trust was gone forever, she would have left him when the affair came out. But that ship sank long ago. Gwen had no job, no family for a thousand miles, and no matter how hard she tried, she hadn't been able to picture raising physically-emotionally-mentally-exhausting Raleigh without Matt to relieve her when he came home. She suspected Matt stuck with her for similar, or at least complementary, reasons. They'd recently marked their thirteenth wedding anniversary. Theirs had become a long, silent marriage.

But this fight was not about Gwen's past—it was about Raleigh's future. Gwen knew she'd failed during Raleigh's infancy because she'd been too tired to fight for Raleigh's sleep when he was a baby. Even now, he woke up in the night several times a week and roused Matt for this or that nonsense, often waking Gwen in the process. But Gwen had a few years of (comparatively) decent sleep in her now that Raleigh was nine, and this was something Gwen, as a teacher, was trained to do: educate a child. So, she opposed Matt until he realized she would never give in.

It was around that time Gwen had Raleigh screened for ADHD. Gwen's younger brother Todd had ADHD, and she saw a lot of Todd in Raleigh—both his learning difficulties as well as his impulsive behavior. But where Todd had been an easy-going boy, Raleigh evinced anger—the base of which Gwen chose not to probe. Threatening to hold him back had been the last straw at the public elementary school. Raleigh had been expelled from public preschool for stabbing a teacher in the hand with a pencil. He had been quietly asked to leave a private, Christian kindergarten for punching two little girls in the face. Gwen had had to write notes of apology and have Raleigh sign them to keep the girls' families from filing lawsuits. Raleigh's teachers at his public elementary school contacted her often to tell of his misdeeds: "Raleigh started a fight;" "Raleigh smashed his classmate's banana into her face;" "Raleigh pushed his classmate off the jungle gym." Raleigh did something remarkable at school at least once a week. His teachers were doubtless relieved when Gwen decided to have him educated elsewhere.

Gwen knew he was different. She'd known since he was a very little baby that he was harder to parent than other people's kids. The hardest part for Gwen was knowing how smart he was for all that he tested poorly. When Gwen read to him—which she did most afternoons while he built ships with LEGOs—he answered her plot and prediction questions well, and by the third grade, he was asking questions of his own. When he was six, she read Dumas' *The Three Musketeers* to him—a six-hundred-page book written at an eighth-grade level. He loved the story and begged her to keep reading even if she'd been at it for an hour or more. Once, he stopped her at the word 'musket' and said: "Musket? What's that? No wait, let me guess: a soldier is carrying it on guard—it's a gun!" Gwen used to spend all year every year trying to impart that very skill to her high school students, and here was her second-grader who could read no more than a few words for himself deducing a word's meaning from context. And yet his teachers checked the "Unsatisfactory" box for Progress in Reading Skills on his report cards.

Gwen also fought to put him in a "hippie" school where the teachers did not assign grades and children advanced according to their unique, personal goals—not according to test scores or school district calendars—because she could not let Raleigh quit school the way Todd had.

In the middle of the third grade, Todd's teacher grew so frustrated with his chattiness, she arranged for him to spend the rest of the school year in the guidance counselor's office, learning only that teachers were allowed to give up on students. She remembered Todd never tried in school after that. Only *their* parents hadn't been teachers—they'd been high school-educated immigrants struggling to pay the mortgages on their American dreams—so Todd wasn't diagnosed with ADHD until his twenties, and had led, thus far, an erratic and penurious life.

The nurse called Gwen back.

"Give Mommy a kiss for good luck," Gwen said, presenting her cheek to Raleigh.

"Good luck, Mommy!" Raleigh said, kissing it. "What if I need the bathroom?"

"It's right through that door," Gwen pointed at the door.

"Okay, good luck."

"Thanks, Baby."

The nurse—a petite, plump woman in her fifties—smiled kindly at Gwen. "My goodness, where are you from?" She said as she weighed Gwen. "You're so tall and thin. You look like a model."

"Thank you." Gwen couldn't help but think anyone younger than sixty and lighter than 200 pounds might look like a model to someone who worked in this doctor's office. But it was true:

Gwen was attractive. She had been a model when she met Matt in their freshman year of college. She looked like all the other Colombian women in her family and did not stand out much back home in South Florida where so many Latinos lived. She and Matt had settled in the Midwest, though, because it was where Matt had been offered the best job and because it was where his family lived—and here locals thought her an "exotic" beauty. She expected "the pretty" (as she thought of it) to fade at any moment and marveled that she was the only person who seemed to notice the gray hairs amid her long, brown curls. She observed every new crease around her eyes and the beginnings of parentheses around her mouth with curiosity and dread. She'd be sorry when the pretty left her, yet she wondered what her face would look like in ten, twenty, forty years—if she lived that long.

Her mother wore a minimum of wrinkles in her mid-fifties, and with her beauty intact she often passed for a younger woman. But Gwen did not have her mother's youthful character. Where Gwen's mother could turn anything into a game and identified most strongly with children younger than ten, Gwen had been the kind of child who thought most children were childish and stupid; she had longed to grow up and talk with adults about serious things. By the time Gwen was fourteen, she was drinking coffee, reading the paper, and plotting her escape from childhood. But now, at thirty-three, though people still remarked on her looks, she knew she would not age into her mother's face.

Which left her father's face.

During the twenty minutes between when the nurse left and the doctor came in, Gwen had plenty of time to think about her father's face. Her father's heart quit when Gwen was twenty-eight. He died at fifty-two; completely white-haired with deep lines, multiple bankruptcies, and two failed marriages on his face. Gwen tried to shake his life-beaten visage from her mind but couldn't. Her parentheses would deepen into his. If she stayed in her unhappy marriage, she would surely acquire the same furrow between her eyes, the same bags beneath them. The pouches under her eyes would make her look sad. She'd read somewhere that bags under the eyes indicated 'unshed tears.' Gwen knew everyday happiness was rare among realists, but it wasn't just that Gwen wasn't happy: she was miserable. The only lines she had started were her crow's feet which might not get someone onto the cover of *Cosmo*, but smile lines were okay. Gwen found them appealing. Gwen sighed.

She and Matt had made each other smile and laugh so much in the beginning. They'd frisked like puppies in college—studying, listening to live alternative rock bands, taking long car trips to visit the ocean. The smiles and laughter had lasted through the first three years of their marriage. They'd graduated, mocked the suits they had to wear for work, and raced home at night to undress each other. But then Matt accepted The Promotion: it was then, Gwen knew now, that she'd lost him. From that day, Matt's mind lived at work. Always. Gwen had felt it first in his hurried lovemaking, then in his lack of interest in lovemaking, then in everything else. Gwen conceived Raleigh by accident one of the three times they'd had sex the fall after The Promotion, but they'd both embraced the idea of parenthood. Gwen had missed being Matt's world, but she'd still believed, deep down, things would get better. Only they didn't. Gwen grew lonely enough that, after a year of failed efforts to gain his attention, including asking him to see a marriage counselor with her, Gwen stopped trying. Raleigh arrived. Life grew harder, messier, and lonelier still. Gwen went back to work so she could talk to someone other than the baby. Matt worked later and talked even less. Eventually, Gwen stopped pining for Matt.

It was then that Frank had started making her laugh every day. Frank, who would have rearranged the stars to talk to Gwen. Gwen fought the memory of Frank's smile and how much she missed it.

Smile lines? Gwen shook her head. Her smiles sprang from politeness these days—unless Raleigh did something charming; then she smiled for real.

The doctor entered the examining room. He was neither old nor young and had the kind of face it was easy to forget—a bland, white face. He listened to Gwen's heart and lungs, then put his stethoscope to her abdomen to listen to her digestive noises. He pressed her stomach lightly. Gwen winced. They discussed her IBS.

"I'm writing you a prescription for a corticosteroid which should bring down the inflammation that's causing your symptoms. If it works—"

"What do you mean 'if'?"

"Every therapy does not work for every patient. If it did, my job would be very easy. We should try this medication first because it's the one that usually works for your problem, and it has the fewest side effects."

"What if it doesn't work?"

"Then we'll try something else."

"Will I be sick forever?" She felt as though she'd already been sick forever—sick in the head, sick in the heart, sick in the gut. If the doctor answered "yes" that would be at least two forever's of stomach pain, bloody diarrhea, and sadness—and Gwen could not bear any more tests. *How*, she wondered, *did old people endure it all?*

"Some people go into remission after starting on an effective therapy."

Gwen considered this. "But some people don't."

"It's a chronic disease."

"I'm afraid, Doctor." Gwen felt very young all of a sudden— young enough to believe in God. She prayed. Gwen hadn't prayed since middle school, but she needed to believe in something. She needed to believe in God. She needed to believe in this doctor.

"There are things you can do," he said, a smile alighting briefly on his face. "Lifestyle changes you can make that might help." Judging from the few creases on his face, this doctor smiled more than he frowned.

Gwen took a pad and pen from her purse. "Such as?"

"Avoid alcohol."

"I don't drink."

"Okay, that's good. Avoid caffeine."

"Are you serious?" What would life be without coffee? If it were a simpler choice such as quick death versus never drinking coffee again, Gwen's fast choice would be death.

"I know, I know. I like coffee, too."

"You don't understand, Doctor. I'm Colombian. My blood is A positive dark roast."

The doctor laughed. Good. If she could make the doctor laugh, then she knew he was listening when she spoke. It was a trick she'd used on her students back when she taught high school—back before Matt insisted she quit because he didn't want her working with Frank. Before Matt called the principal and the head of her department to tell them why Gwen quit. Before the small town they lived in decided Gwen wasn't welcome there after all. Before the economy died and they started laying teachers off instead of hiring them. Before she'd spent seven years looking, unsuccessfully, for full-time work. Shit. Gwen couldn't think about that now. She'd fall apart if she did.

"Give decaf a try. Also, try to eat frequent, smaller meals."

Gwen swallowed. "I can do that."

"I know you exercise." He took off his glasses, wiped them with his tie, and said, "You're a runner, right?"

Gwen nodded.

"Stop."

"You're kidding."

"I'm not saying *not* to exercise but running jolts your internal organs around. And your intestines might like it better if you took up something low impact."

"Okay." Gwen didn't love running so much as she loved the muscles she got from it. She could do Pilates if she had to. She sighed. The Pilates women at her gym all had nannies and important careers.

"Now here's the toughie," he said.

"Tougher than giving up coffee and running? What? Do I need to bring peace to the Middle East?"

"Maybe."

Gwen gave the doctor her most helpless look.

He said: "A reduction in stress almost always leads to remission."

Gwen worked at not rolling her eyes. She ultimately had to close them to keep from rolling them. Give up stress? Wouldn't she love to? Wouldn't everyone? Was this calm, bland-faced man out of his mind? Gwen said nothing.

The doctor went on: "I can't help you with that. You already eat well and exercise. I see in your chart that you're on antidepressants. You do take them? Every day?"

Gwen nodded yes.

"And you talk to someone?"

She felt close to tears. Her psychiatrist was about the only person Gwen could talk to.

"So maybe there's some decision you're putting off or some secret you're holding in..." Dr. Anderson didn't finish the sentence. It was not quite a question, though it lacked the certainty of a statement.

Gwen felt tears falling off her eyelashes.

"I thought so." Dr. Anderson shifted in his seat. "I'm not the right doctor for this sort of thing. But I want you to get better, Gwen. And medical science is turning up more and more evidence of the mind-body connection." He handed her a box of tissues.

"Thanks, Doctor."

He printed something and gave it to her. "Here's your prescription. Good luck with the coffee and," his voice softened, "with peace in the Middle East. I want to see you back here in three weeks."

Gwen folded the prescription and put it in her purse. She walked as fast as she could to the bathroom. Raleigh had been on his own in the waiting room for half an hour. That was half an eternity in Raleigh Time. But she needed to compose herself before she saw him. The bathroom door was locked. Gwen knocked. Somebody flushed. The door opened. There stood Raleigh looking up at Gwen's teary face.

He pulled her down to hug her. "Poor Mommy!" he said. "Did the doctor give you a shot?" He smoothed her hair and kissed her cheek. "It hurts when they do that." He kissed her cheek again, then stepped back, looking at her with his head cocked to one side. A moment later he took a Lifesaver from his pocket and held it out. "I was saving this for later, but if you want it, you can have it."

"Where'd you get that?" Gwen asked, laughing her tears off. She didn't let Raleigh have candy unless it was Halloween, or he'd just had a shot.

"The lady at the front desk gave it to me."

Gwen gave him a stern look.

"I was gonna ask you if it was okay before I ate it."

And he probably would have. He was not a devious child. In addition to not being devious, Raleigh had no poker face. The few times he tried pulling one over on Gwen, she busted him pretty much instantly. Gwen wondered if he'd stay freakishly honest all his life or if he'd learn to lie like everyone else.

"It was incredibly sweet of you to offer it to me, but you keep it. You can have it after lunch."

"Okay, Mommy. I got you to stop crying. Did ya know—"

Gwen turned her attention to the receptionist, who was asking her questions about a follow-up appointment. Raleigh kept on talking.

"I'm sorry, Baby. I have to give this lady my attention. I need to make an appointment to come back."

"More shots?" Raleigh's eyes grew round and solemn. "Are you gonna be okay, Mommy?"

"He's a very good doctor. Now, please," she caressed his ear, "I need to make this appointment."

The receptionist looked as though she'd already spent the last of her patience on Raleigh, and she wasn't keen on going into debt to make it through this transaction. "In the future, Mrs. Goddard, it might be best to leave the young one at home."

Gwen smiled her most polite smile and said, "Yes, of course."

She did not say, "Bitch." Though she ended so many sentences that way, always silently.

Once in the car, Gwen said, "You survived the waiting room. I'm proud of you."

"Oh, Mommy," Raleigh said, "I know why that lady didn't want me to come back."

"Why?"

"Because I accidentally spilled my juice on the chair."

"Did you clean it up?"

"I tried. I used the little towel you put in the Everything Bag. But the lady was still upset."

"Did you say you were sorry?"

"Yes!"

"Cleaning up and apologizing is about all you can do when you make a mess." *And sometimes,* Gwen thought but did not say, *there is nothing you can do to make it better.*

"She looked at me like she wanted to open her mouth and breathe fire at me and watch me turn to ashes."

"I'm sure she did." Gwen allowed herself a small laugh. "And I'm laughing at your description, Baby, not at the mess or the dragon lady."

It was Raleigh's turn to laugh.

They approached a large intersection. The light turned red. Gwen stopped and waited. The light turned green. Gwen pressed the accelerator. Nothing. Then the car died right there in the center lane. The drivers of the four cars behind her took turns leaning on their horns, then passing her—a diverted river of angry gestures.

"Mommy, go! Why didn't you go? The light was green." He paused briefly. "Mommy?"

"The car won't go. It's broken."

"That's bad. Everyone's mad at us. I saw their faces when they passed us. They were really, really mad."

"Yes, Baby."

"What are you going to do?"

"I have to push the car to the side of the road and call someone to help us."

"You're strong enough to push a car?"

The awe in Raleigh's tone pushed Gwen's tears back inside her head, and she laughed instead.

"Can I help?"

"If you were older, I'd *make* you help."

"You mean like if I were in high school?" He sat up straighter and taller in his seat.

"Yes.

"Listen, Baby, I have to move the car now. You just stay where you are."

Gwen put the car in neutral, then walked behind it and pushed. The ground was slick. She fell. She stood up, wet-kneed and angry, and tried to push from a different angle. She caught herself before falling this time. The car was halfway between the middle and right lanes. She couldn't push too hard without anyone to steer, otherwise, she risked pushing it into oncoming traffic. Gwen cursed winter. Had it been summer, with her long legs on display in a pair of shorts, she would have the help of three men to push her car by now. But besides being immured in her parka, it was seven degrees outside—much too cold for casual Samaritanism. The best she could hope for was a police officer, but none appeared.

After eleven minutes of pushing, falling, and steering, the car was on the shoulder. Gwen's fingers felt like they might snap off, and the car's heater stopped working when the engine died.

"I'm cold, Mommy."

"Me, too, Baby." Gwen scanned the street. Wherever they went had to be close. Raleigh had left his hat and gloves at home, and while Gwen had a spare hat, she could only find one spare left-hand glove for him. The area was mostly farmland, but there was a small plaza across the street.

"We are going to walk to that building across the street." Gwen pointed to it. "And get warm in there while I call for help."

"How long will it take?"

"I don't know."

"Will Daddy come to get us?" Raleigh said hopefully, then added, "No offense, but he's more fun than you."

They were on the street now, waiting for the light to change so they could cross. Trucks whooshed past.

"None taken," Gwen lied. "But I don't know if Daddy will get us."

"I hope Daddy gets us."

"Me, too." Gwen wasn't sure if this last statement was true or not but figured it was true enough. If Matt came to get them, the day would probably be easier. But Gwen wasn't in the mood for the lecture he'd give her for not noticing the check engine light sooner. Her stomach hurt too much. She didn't understand why things always had to be someone's fault with Matt.

They crossed the street to a plaza with three storefronts: a pizza place that didn't open for four hours, one "Available for Lease," and a dry-cleaner. Jesus. Could there be a more boring place to take Raleigh? At least it would be warm.

The bell attached to the door announced their arrival. A gray-haired lady came to the counter. "Hello," she said. "How can I help you?"

"Hi, ma'am. I'm Gwen, and this is Raleigh." Gwen put her

hand out, and the lady shook it. "You see that car across the street? The blue one off to the side? That's our car. It broke down."

"Oh, that's bad luck."

"Yes. And it's freezing outside. My little boy is cold, so I hoped we could stay here until help comes."

"Of course. No problem."

"Thank you."

The lady returned to the back of the store.

"She's nice," Raleigh said.

"She is," Gwen agreed.

Gwen called Matt. Her first try went straight to voicemail. Gwen did not need any more challenges today. She'd had her fill. She needed to be rescued. Now.

She called again.

"I'm in a meeting."

"Hi."

"What do you need?"

"The car broke down. We're out by my doctor's office. We're at least ten miles from the dealer and fifteen from home."

"I can't leave work right now. Call AAA."

"They only cover a tow if it's within five miles of the shop."

"Call them anyway. Or call around. I have to get back to the meeting."

"Love you," Gwen said into the click of Matt hanging up.

Gwen put her phone down and pressed her temples with her fingers. The smell of the dry-cleaning chemicals had already given her a headache. It was so bad she nearly forgot about the cutlery in her gut.

Raleigh came to where Gwen sat and put his hand on her shoulder.

Had he been talking all this time and she'd tuned him out? Or had he been uncharacteristically silent? Gwen hated herself for not knowing.

"Mommy," Raleigh said.

"Yes, Baby?"

"Am I being good?"

"Yes, you are, Son. Thank you."

"I'm trying really hard." He squeezed his hands into tight fists as if to demonstrate how hard he was trying.

Gwen kissed his cheek—how she loved kissing his cheeks. "You're the best."

Raleigh smiled. "Did you know melting icebergs can flip upside down?"

"No, I didn't know that."

"Daddy can't get us, can he?"

"No, he can't leave work."

"That stinks."

"Yes, it does. And now I have to ask you to be really quiet and not touch anything while I call around and get us some help."

"Okay, Mommy."

So, Raleigh went back to his book of amazing facts, and Gwen called for a tow truck. The truck arrived a miraculous fifteen minutes later. Having a car towed to a repair shop, Gwen knew, put her at the complete mercy of the mechanics, so she resolved to make it as painless as possible for Raleigh, at least.

Raleigh loved fast-food hamburgers more than any other victuals. Like candy, Gwen didn't allow him to eat them more than two or three times a year—on her watch, anyway (but when Raleigh called Matt "fun" he meant, among other things, that Matt let him eat whatever he wanted). Also, since Gwen did not consider drive-through hamburgers food, she never ate them. But it was lunchtime, and who knew how long they'd be stuck at the repair shop with nothing but exhaust fumes and sticky magazines. This was an emergency.

"Can we drive through somewhere and get a couple of burgers on the way to the shop?" Gwen asked the tow truck driver. Before the tow truck driver could answer, Raleigh spoke: "My mommy's really sick. We just came from her doctor. He gave her a shot, so she was crying when she came out, and now she wants a hamburger. My mommy never eats hamburgers. Never. She must be really sick. Are you that sick, Mommy?"

Gwen just looked at the tow truck driver and begged with her eyes.

The tow truck driver coughed into one of his rough hands. "There's a Burger King a few miles up. You guys can get lunch there, ma'am. Won't add any to your bill."

"Mommy?"

"Yes, Baby?"

"You didn't answer my question."

Gwen looked out at the piles of gray-brown snow framing the road. "I am sick enough to buy us burgers, Son."

That night, after agreeing to $2,178.77 of repairs; after spending five hours in the mechanic's shop listening to stupid soap operas emanate from the TV; after playing twenty questions eight times with Raleigh; after learning that a Komodo dragon can swallow a goat whole and that snakes don't have eyelids, and sharks can't blink, and flamingoes don't turn pink until they're two years old, and a group of ravens is called an unkindness; after declining the mechanic's offer to lower the price of replacing her alternator, timing belt, and brake pads if she'd have dinner with him the following night; after Matt finally picked them up; after having no time to fill her prescription; after a dinner lecture on proper car care; after putting Raleigh to bed; after a much-needed bath; and after eight years of feeling sick all over, Gwen lay awake in bed next to Matt who she knew would be snoring soon. Matt never had trouble sleeping. Gwen, on the other hand, slept, at best, like a fugitive from the law: even when she fell asleep within an hour of going to bed, she was hunted in her dreams.

"Matt," Gwen whispered loudly.

"Hmmm?"

"Can we talk?"

"Now?"

Gwen knew other couples talked at night. Some even talked like friends. Gwen thought with a stab of memory of the last time she'd talked companionably in bed with a man: it had been with Frank. It had been seven years since Gwen had spoken companionably with a man in bed.

Gwen's body felt cold under the down comforter. "Now," she said.

Matt didn't move. "What is it?"

"When was the last time I made you happy?"

"Gwen," he started, but didn't finish.

"When, Matt? When was the last time you thought to yourself: 'I'm a lucky guy to be married to Gwen'?"

Gwen remembered Frank's jealousy of Matt. How he'd said, "Matt's a lucky guy to be married to you."

"What is this about?" Matt sounded annoyed.

"Have you noticed we don't even speak in declarative sentences anymore? That we ask questions instead of saying what we think?"

Gwen felt Matt's body tense up next to her.

"You want me to stop asking you questions?"

Gwen's face grew hot, and she could hear her pulse in her ears. She said, "Just tell me the last time you felt lucky to be married to me."

"Honestly?"

"No, Matt. Lie to me." She knew her sarcasm would make him angry, but she didn't care.

"Honestly, Gwen, it's been a while."

"Like how long?"

Seven years? Eight? He'd stopped listening to her eight years ago.

"You're amazing with Raleigh. You have more patience than I do with him. That makes me happy to be with you."

"Okay." Gwen's tears fell soundlessly onto her pillow. She steadied her voice. "I appreciate how you are with Raleigh, too. His first thought after we got stuck today was that he hoped *you* would come to get us—because you're more fun." *But,* she thought but didn't say, *Raleigh will grow up. Then what?*

"I was in a meeting. You handled it."

She had, hadn't she? Though it was Matt who would pay the bill.

"I know. But besides my mothering—what do you like about me?"

Matt paused. Gwen waited.

Matt said, "You're gorgeous."

He said that was something he liked about her—and he had liked it in the beginning—but since the affair, he checked up on her any time she went somewhere looking especially pretty without him, texting several times an hour and becoming enraged if she failed to answer his texts promptly. Her beauty did not make Matt happy.

"What if I were in an accident and horribly disfigured?"

"What are you getting at, Gwen?"

His tone made Gwen's insides feel like glass in a garbage disposal. Condescension. He used a condescending tone when he spoke to her—not just at this moment, but all the time.

"Ask me. Ask me when I last felt lucky to be married to you."

Matt sat up in the dark. Gwen heard him breathing hard. "When was the last time you felt lucky to be married to me, Gwen?"

There was anger in his voice now.

"Aside from your fathering, it's been years."

The fact that Gwen had stayed all these years—in part because she didn't think she could manage Raleigh on her own—made Gwen feel weak. It felt to her as if she depended on Matt for everything. How had she let such a thing happen?

"Aren't you forgetting something?" Matt hissed. "Aren't you forgetting the nice lifestyle I give you? Summers in South America are nice, aren't they, Gwen? The Lexus you drive; it's nice? The nice shoes bursting out of every closet in the house? It's nice, too, I bet, to charge *anything you want* on a credit card and never get a bill. Isn't it? Tell me that's not the biggest reason you've stayed."

Gwen blinked but didn't answer. They weren't questions. The fact that all her attempts at earning enough money to support even the most basic lifestyle had failed was the sharpest pain in Gwen's body. If her ten-year-old self could see how Gwen's life had turned out, she was sure the girl would die of rage, and if Gwen had looked for happiness in spending Matt's money, it was because she'd looked everywhere else first and come away empty-hearted.

"Huh, Gwen? No denial?" He was nearly shouting. "You

realize that makes you a whore?"

"Lower your voice," Gwen said.

"Don't tell me what to do!" Matt shouted.

"Raleigh will be in here in a minute unless you lower your voice."

"Let him come!" Matt yelled. "Let him hear what a lazy whore his mother is!"

Gwen heard Raleigh sobbing outside their bedroom door. She stood up.

"I'm going into the hall to take care of Raleigh," Gwen said quietly. "I won't be coming back in here, so I'm just going to say what I have to say right now: I need a divorce."

Gwen left the bedroom and found Raleigh steeped in tears. She made him a cup of warm milk with honey, read "Stopping by the Woods on a Snowy Evening" with him, and tucked him back into bed.

"Mommy," he said, his voice still shaking, "I don't want you and Daddy to fight anymore. It makes me mad and gives me nightmares."

She hoped the darkness of Raleigh's room hid her tears.

He went on: "You don't love Daddy like I do. I can tell."

Gwen sat speechless at the edge of Raleigh's bed.

He sat up and hugged her very tightly. "I love you, Mommy."

"And I love you," she said, kissing Raleigh's temple, "more than anything." In the dark like this, he had a baby-ness to him that he hadn't had in the light since he was three. Gwen put her face in his curls. They'd coarsened since he was a baby, but they were still very soft.

"You love me more than *anything*?"

Gwen gave silent thanks for his short attention span.

"More than anything, Raleigh."

"More than books?"

"More than books."

Raleigh reached for Gwen's hand, lacing his skinny fingers in hers. "More than poems?" He asked.

Gwen squeezed his fingers. "More than poems."

With that, Raleigh said "Wow" and put his head back on his pillow. Gwen stayed until he was asleep.

She crept out of his room, quiet as a feather, made up the guest bed, and, surprisingly, fell right to sleep. Her last dream before waking was of nursing a baby girl.

The Evil Vortex of Doom

The last time I saw my father alive, I was visiting my twin, Tom, in Manhattan. Tom said, "Let's get lunch in Queens." My vagabond brother, a D.J. who had taken an apartment in Midtown as soon as adulthood set in, baited his lunch-in-Queens trap with tantalizing words: 'Gino's Pizza' and 'cheesecake from Damiano's.' I'd been away from the motherland so long I *needed* some authentic Gino's pizza.

Tom took the Lincoln Tunnel.

I said, "This isn't the way to Queens."

We were born in Queens. We'd lived there until we lost half of our baby teeth and Mom got sick of winter. She was happier in Miami (except for missing her mom and dad). We returned most summers during our childhood for long visits with our grandparents in Queens, but they died when Tom and I were sixteen. I hadn't been back since their funerals. Ten years was a long time—though not so long I didn't remember which way was Queens.

"We're going to Rutherford." He said this staring straight ahead like he was focused on his driving or bracing himself for a blow.

"Turn around. You promised me Queens. Gino's. Damiano's."

"I'm taking you to see Dad."

I punched his arm. He winced like it hurt, out of respect. We're twins: same brown eyes, same curly brown hair, Mom's light olive skin. Only Tom got Dad's massive, polar-bear physique, and I am built more like our mother which is to say I'm tall and thin but with all the musculature of a naked eyelash. And I'm a woman. My hardest punch could only hope to annoy my brother's treelike arm.

I'd gone to visit Tom to drag myself out of the bog sand of my depression because Tom and I share, above all, a sense of humor. No matter how old we get, we're always the same two little kids laughing in the same sandbox. But I should have known he'd become our father's Agent of Doom—he lived too close to the old man not to be. I should have known, too, because spending time with my family never goes according to my plans.

**

I was nineteen, for example, the time Dad sent me a plane ticket to Mérida so I could meet my stepmother and step-siblings. It had been a year since he'd divorced Mom; ten months since he'd married Adabella. I went because Tom was in Mérida working for Dad—not because I was dying to meet Dad's replacement family.

College expenses had pauperized me, and I hadn't seen Tom in six months. It was the longest I'd gone without seeing him, and I missed him so much that everything I ate tasted like raw potatoes.

Dad knew this and used it to lure me to Mexico—told me Tom loved Mérida; that it was hot like Miami but ancient and charming; that they wanted to show me the Mayan ruins. Ruins? Yes.

It was the maid's day off. Adabella was in the kitchen making dinner. Dad and I sat at the sparkling, glass-top dining-room table. I watched his reflection. He watched me.

I said, "Dad, give me your phone number so I can call you."

"I'll give it to you, Honey, under one condition," Dad said.

(Mmmm, conditional love!)

"What?"

"You can't give it to your mother."

Mom deserved a shiny gold halo and a choir of harp-wielding seraphim—or at least alimony—for having been married to Dad for twenty years. She didn't even have his phone number?

"I won't promise that."

"Then call me at the *maquila*." His jewelry factory. The one he moved to Mexico.

"You never answer the phone there."

"I know. But I get the messages."

My tiny, Mexican stepmother came out of the kitchen with two plates of food: steaks and fried potatoes piled artfully on lime green dishes, garnished with carrots carved to resemble flowers with homemade *chimichurri* on the side. She served ours, then returned to the kitchen for her plate.

I'd wanted to hate my stepmother but couldn't. When I developed a fever and sore throat the first day of my visit, she brought me tea and lemon juice with honey. She fussed over me for three days until I got well. She offered me aspirin, sent the younger children (she had four from her first marriage) to stay at their father's house, and even threatened to call a doctor. She smelled like chamomile and laundry soap. She smiled at me with affection. Adabella was, in mien and mood, just like my mother.

She reappeared, plate in hand. She sat across from Dad.

Dad picked up his fork, inspected it, and made his furious Henry VIII face. "This fork is filthy! How could you put this on the table? Really, *mi amor*, what's wrong with you?"

Adabella stood, went back to the kitchen.

"Dad!" I hissed. "You shouldn't talk that way to anybody, let alone your wife. I thought you liked Adabella."

"Look!" He held up the offending utensil. "There's a tomato seed stuck on this fork. It's really disgusting."

Adabella came out of the kitchen. "*Buen provecho*, Lexie," she said to me, car keys in hand. Then, to Dad, she said, "I'm going to get the kids from Emilio. Have you seen my purse, *mi amor*?"

The way they said *mi amor* in Spanish could freeze the Gulf of Mexico.

"It's probably in the car. This place is such a disaster; I'm not surprised you lost it. You'd lose your head if it wasn't screwed on!"

"Dad!" I said, pointlessly, robbed of all hunger.

This is how I remember it. Maybe he didn't use those exact words. Dad traveled between creative insults: 'You know why you're so dangerous? Because you're an idiot with initiative!' and the 'if it wasn't screwed on' kind. He didn't discriminate based on the occasion. He'd called sixteen-year-old Tom an 'oozing pus-brain' after Tom had tried to hide a ding he'd made in the door of Dad's prized Mercedes. He'd called me a 'cock-teaser' once when I came home late from work the summer between high school and college. He wasn't wrong.

I'd crossed the stage at my high school 'graduation' only to be handed a blank diploma case—my father had failed to pay tuition my entire senior year. It was going to cost four thousand dollars to think about starting my own life.

So, while my fellow alumni interned or life-guarded or performed wanton wardrobe expansions with their employee discounts at The Gap, I ransomed my high school diploma one lap dance at a time. I was, in fact, Supreme Cabaret's cock-teaser extraordinaire. But Dad didn't know about my job. I'd told him my friend refused to drive me home from a night out after I flirted with her latest love interest. He was insulting my pretext for coming home so late, not my actual, stripperly self.

"Sorry, Lexie," said Dad, wiping the tomato seed off his fork.

"Don't apologize to me."

"She's so careless." He waved, palm up, at her retreating shadow. "It's frustrating."

He used to say the same thing about Mom in more or less the same words. Living with us had been a breaking wheel for him. Mom was an indifferent housekeeper. Tom and I were slobs. Once, when we were on vacation and the police responded to our burglar alarm (a hail stone had come through the living room window), they wrote in the report, 'kids' bedrooms ransacked.'

I impaled a potato with my fork. "Face it, Dad." I sighed. "You dig careless chicks."

Dad lit a cigarette. Then he fixed me with his ursine smile. "Tom will be here soon."

***

Dad had fled to Rutherford to be near Tom after he lost the *maquila* in a bet and Adabella kicked him out. So, Tom kidnapped me to Jersey.

"Why, Tom? Why would you do this to me?"

How far had I run from our father? All the way to Iowa. Jeff, my soon-to-be-ex-husband, had been a graduate student at the university I'd attended in Miami.

We met in the elevator before my Shakespeare class my freshman year. We stood at antipodes, sneaking looks at each other in wordless attraction the first time, uncustomarily grateful the elevator in Row Hall was the slowest in the New

World. The second time, I stuck out my hand and said, "Hi, I'm Lexie." The third time we shared the elevator, he invited me for a cup of coffee. Two months later, I told him where I worked and why. He said, "That's sad." Before returning to Iowa City with his Ph.D. (my junior year), he said, "I wish you'd come to Iowa with me." No more stripping, he meant but didn't say. I moved to Iowa and into an apartment with Jeff. I continued school there. No more dancing.

I missed my mother. And Miami. Or I'd forgotten how to smile? Not that I didn't try—but my smiles were all teeth, no soul. I wore long wool skirts that itched. People kept telling me, "You look so serious for someone your age."

I married Jeff the summer before my senior year of college. Nothing in my disorderly childhood, it seemed, had prepared me for the bland stability of being Jeff's wife. I kept waiting for a disaster to blow it all up: a crazy ex-lover, a tornado, the Law to come to take Jeff away. But nothing did. I graduated. We bought a house in the 'burbs. I even took a job teaching tenth-grade English to a bunch of corn-blond Iowan kids who hated *The Catcher in the Rye*.

Four years ago, by miracle or mistake, Jeff and I had a son— Julian. I went from looking serious to sporting what my father, had he been there to see me, would've called 'funeral face.' At first, it might have been hormones—after that, the desperation I felt had no easy excuse. I cried every time I changed a diaper. I went around believing things like, 'I wish I were dead,' and 'I hate my life,' and 'What kind of stupid God thought *I* should be a mother?' I slept when I should have stayed awake and spent the sleeping hours counting black sheep.

My maternity leave ended *(Things could've gotten better)*. Feeling invisible, I went to work in low-cut blouses and miniskirts *(Would they see me now?)*. One morning, after several breakfast brandies, I showed up in an old dancing costume: a thong-bottomed Wonder Woman outfit—complete with power wristbands and a gold Lasso of Truth—and threw up in First hour. My students carried me to the principal's office. Little daisy-faced Katie Bean, said, "Mr. Hein, Mrs. Dunn is sick. I think she needs a doctor."

After the firing, my co-worker, Ruth, loaned me her walking coat. She helped me carry my dictionaries, Thoreau posters, and coffee mug to my car. Then she drove me home.

Ruth shook her head, repeating, "Why not just quit?"

I said, "I might."

I didn't kill myself because, if I died, who in Iowa would teach Julian that Spanish was not just the language of housemaids and busboys? A stupid reason, maybe, but I wasn't operating at the top of my reason.

I was alive, technically, but my libido was long dead. Jeff said, "Are we ever having sex again?"

I said, "You have your sex and I have mine."

Jeff worked longer and longer hours with his research assistant, Debbie. I'd never met Debbie, but we'd talked on the phone once or twice. I could tell from her voice that she smiled a lot.

Julian kept growing and doing things like crawling into the study and teething on the collectors' edition of Hemingway's *The Short Stories* that Tom had gotten me for my twenty-sixth birthday. I would put Julian in the stroller and walk for hours— or stay in and read *Memories of My Melancholy Whores* to him, in Spanish, while he wailed—to keep myself this side of oblivion. Mom told me motherhood is always hard and that I should stay tough. Tom told me I should see someone. I said, "I'm married.

I see someone every day." Jeff kept making me doctors' appointments. I kept not going to them.

Jeff stopped talking to me. He grunted—unless it was about Julian. We spoke in complete sentences to one another only if it was about the baby.

One morning I woke up, late as usual, to an odd silence: Jeff and Julian were gone. A note said Julian was at my mother and father-in-law's house, and Jeff wanted a separation because I was, as he put it, 'a disaster.'

I was the crazy ex-lover/tornado/Law Man?

Then I had the terrifying thought that prompted the call to the counseling center ("I need to talk to someone who specializes in women whose children have been taken away, who have marital problems and invisibility problems, who drink too much, and who are very, very serious.") The thought: Julian could grow up to hate me.

I knew from experience that children could grow up to hate their parents.

***

Halfway into my senior year of high school, a year before Dad filed for divorce, he asked me to help him shop for a birthday gift for Mom. Mom would turn thirty-nine in a week. I'd already bought her a yummy, pink terrycloth bathrobe. I'd even had it embroidered with her initials. I'd had to babysit our neighbors' three rowdy kids every Saturday night for a month, but the robe was thick and soft, and Mom's old one was a hole shy of becoming a dishrag—and Mom hadn't bought herself anything new in years.

For the last four years, Dad had stayed in Mexico more and more, and so had his paychecks. We missed them both. Mom had just been laid off. Again. Sometimes we lived without electricity. Sometimes we lived without running water. We played a daily game of hide-the-car-from-the-repo-man. Creditors called and called and called. But that was my parents' concern, or so I thought. I'd bought Mom the robe thinking it would be inappropriate for me to offer to pay the electric bill.

It seemed typical of Dad to not pay bills but still have cash handy for a gift. I told myself it was romantic of him. I was flattered he wanted my help and was happy to spend time alone with him. Maybe I'd get something, too?

We set out. When Dad said 'shopping' it usually meant a trip to Bal Harbor Shops, CocoWalk, or at least Dolphin Mall. I closed my eyes and imagined myself at the perfume counter, being courted by three or four white-suited saleswomen.

Dad made his turn. I opened my eyes: too many liquor stores, not enough trees, towering graffiti, young men standing at bus stops not waiting for the bus—the kind of neighborhood where you kept the car windows closed no matter the weather. This was the wrong side of town for 'romantic.' Dad pulled up to The Family Pawn Shop.

"Let's go, Lexie," he said, unlocking the car doors.

"You know I hate this place."

Yes, we'd been there before. I refused to unbuckle my seatbelt.

"Oh, c'mon. It'll be quick."

Like ripping off a Band-Aid too soon.

"Why did I have to come?"

Dad unbuckled my seatbelt, saying, "Tito always gives me a better price when you're around."

I looked down at my cut-off jean shorts and sparkly tank top—typical clothes for a teenager in Miami—and sweltered with rage.

We went in. I scowled at Tito (thirty-five, heavily inked, the face and gait of a garden lizard). He and Dad made a minute of small talk. I scowled some more.

"Lexie! So good to see your beautiful smile! I hear you had a birthday. You're legal now." He laughed like this was funny.

So did Dad.

"What can you give me for these, Tito?"

Tito didn't answer; he just gawked at the fray of my shorts.

I looked at what Dad had shaken from a green, velvet bag: my grandmother's diamond and pearl earrings. My earrings! The only thing Mom was able to get for me after her four brothers, their wives, and my cousin, Romina, had taken everything else. The earrings my grandmother had promised to me—the reason why no one else had claimed them.

"You can't have them." I snatched them off the counter. "These are mine."

Dad and Tito looked at me. Dad nodded to Tito. Tito went to straighten the broken engagement ring display in a case several yards away.

I surveyed the ratty brown carpet, the gold posts of my grandmother's earrings digging into my palm, an eye to the door.

"Lexie, Honey, I know how you love those earrings, and you're right, they are yours. That's why I brought you here. I wanted your permission."

"No!" I headed for the door.

He followed me, put a giant paw on my arm. "Lexie, look, we wouldn't be here if we had anything else to pawn. There's nothing left. I sold my guns. Mom's jewelry. My camera equipment. Tom's stereo."

That's what had happened to Tom's stereo? Tom couldn't have agreed to that—he would've sooner sold a gallon of blood.

"I don't care."

"It's just a loan, Lexie. I've got a big order coming in two weeks—but not in time for your mother's birthday. Tito will hold your earrings for three months—longer even if I ask him to. He knows me. As soon as the order comes in, we'll come back for them. Please, Lexie."

"No."

I got to the door but hesitated. I was afraid to sit by myself in a Mercedes-Benz in this neighborhood. I shuffled my feet and looked at Dad.

He took off his wedding band and placed it solemnly on the counter. It made the slightest clink. Tito returned instantly to the counter at the sound.

"You want to pawn *this*, Guillermo?"

Dad looked like he might cry. He didn't say anything. Just stared at the small, gold circle on the counter.

Tito repeated his question.

Dad repeated his silence.

Tom had given up his stereo.

"No, Tito," I said, putting my earrings back on the counter. "Take these."

***

Tom hadn't turned the car around. Traffic was light. The endless square-tiled tunnel walls whizzed past—the red and yellow tunnel lights turning Tom's complexion sallow and ghost-like.

He said, "Dad's really sick."

Our father had his first heart attack at the end of our freshman year of high school. He'd held Tom hostage with one illness or another since the divorce.

We were near the end of the Lincoln Tunnel.

"Really?" I asked. "Let's visit him some other time—when he's well."

Tom kept talking to me. "The cancer is back. And he's been having strokes. Last month he called me to say he couldn't feel his right foot."

"Why the fuck wouldn't he call 911?"

"He says he doesn't want any more doctors."

"Fucking coward."

"He doesn't care if you curse him out."

Daylight was on us now. A big sign read "Welcome to New Jersey."

"He's dying, Alexandra. He wants to see you again before he dies. You'll thank me someday."

"Fuck you very much."

We crossed rivers, a creek, white and brown churches with signs in multiple languages: a thirteen-mile trip.

Welcome to Rutherford: population 18,110—and one captive.

Tom parked behind Trappers Restaurant. I could tell from the clean carpet and the hostess' deferential greeting that it was the kind of restaurant Dad liked—a spic and span kitchen and easily intimidated waitstaff: "Oh that spoon is smudged! How embarrassing. Glad it was you who saw it and not the health inspector. Damn that new dish washer—he's fired! Is this one better? Yes? Good. Dessert is on the house tonight. So sorry." A place with shiny bowls full of heart attack sauces for the fat-laden meats.

Eight years had passed since my dinner with Dad and Adabella. Dad and I hadn't spoken since he offered to pay for my wedding then didn't—and didn't call, write, or answer my phone calls for six months thereafter. It had been almost seven years since we had any contact. Tom said it was because Dad had cancer.

Our father had a form of cancer for every occasion.

Dad was on his best behavior. He asked the hostess to seat us in non-smoking. She looked at him, eyebrows like church steeples, and said, "Are you sure, Bill?" Here he was—Bill. In Mexico, or anywhere Spanish was the lingua franca, he was Guillermo.

"So, how have you been?"

I looked at him, but I didn't smile. I left his question alone.

His hair had gone white, and he wore glasses now. He'd lost at least a hundred pounds. His skin had a yellow tinge. He was fifty-one.

"How's work? You still teaching?"

He had one hand on Tom's arm and one on the table. His hands shook.

I still couldn't speak.

"So, Lex, doesn't Dad look slim? Dad, tell Lexie about your treadmill."

Tom's allergic to silence.

"I walk three miles on it *every day*, Lexie, but it still looks better than I do."

He used to be so big. He and Tom. They'd walked along streets in Mérida like Brobdingnagians in Lilliput. I tried to summon the old rage.

"You'll get there, Dad," I said, unable, even, to muster sarcasm.

"I'd love to see pictures of Julian. Tom forwarded me a few. He's a handsome kid, my grandson."

I pulled a mini photo album—when we were together Jeff used to call them 'brag books'—from my purse. For the first three months of our separation, those brag books were all I saw of Julian from Monday through Saturday. I'd worked my way up (counseling, begging, lawyering-up) to five days a week—still not enough. Handing the book to Tom to hand to Dad was like picking a fresh scab.

Tom and Dad pored over the album together.

Julian was named for Jeff's dad, who was in several of the photos.

Dad pointed to a picture of Julian hugging Jeff's dad at a baseball game. "That must be his other grandfather." Dad took off his glasses, blew his nose, wiped his glasses, and put them back on.

"Julian looks a lot like you, Dad," said Tom.

He did.

Dad said, "I was never that adorable."

He was.

***

I was fourteen when Dad picked me up from my first school dance at Saint Francis of Assisi Catholic Academy in Miami. Tom thought school dances were lame, so he went to a friend's house for the weekend instead. Andrew O'Brien, who was supposed to have been my date, spent the whole night breathing in Jenny Gutierrez's eau d'whore. I'd stood by the punch bowl, watching them slow dance to "The Electric Slide"—my friend, Lisa, offering to lure Jenny outside and hold her down so I could inflict contrition on her. If it hadn't been for the godly presences of Sister Hellawaits and Mother Severo, that might've happened. Instead, I called home, said I was sick, and asked to be picked up. I expected Mom.

Lisa waited outside the parish hall with me. She waved me off when Dad pulled up.

He opened the car door for me. I got in.

"Mom said you were sick." He turned the radio on and fiddled with the dial. "What hurts, Princess?"

"Nothing!" I shouted over the music. "I'm fine."

Had Mom picked me up, I'd have spilled the whole story—wept like at the end of that movie where the young heroine dies of breast cancer. With Dad, it was different. He'd become a distant planet to me since he'd started his business trips to Mexico that summer. And I was changing. It annoyed me that I was somehow half-him but without the persuasive smile and winning laugh. Tom, at least, was a happy caterpillar. I was a quivering larva. I got acne and menstrual periods. I got ditched at the school dance. I was not about to lose it in front of my suave, remote father.

He lowered the volume as we left the parking lot. "What do you want to do now?" he asked.

Hoping he'd laugh and leave me to my misery, I said, "I want to drink wine and go dancing on the beach."

"Okay."

He turned east onto the Rickenbacker Causeway—away from home—towards Miami Beach. I rolled down the window and inhaled; it was a hot, briny smell.

Buildings' reflections shone saber-like in the night-black water of the bay.

We breathed in silence for a while.

"Won't Mom wonder where we are?"

"We'll call her."

We stopped at a gas station. I stayed in the car while he called Mom from the payphone.

Minutes later we pulled into the parking lot of Bolero. I'd never been to a nightclub, but I'd seen them in movies. A neon sign, a line of people waiting to get in, music so loud you could hear it from the parking lot: this was definitely a nightclub.

I could never have passed for eighteen—my grapelike breasts nestled deep in the padding of my first bra—but I was tall and well-dressed for my age. I could have passed for someone old enough to try to pass for eighteen. But I didn't have to. Dad's cop friend, Rico, moonlighted as a doorman at this particular club. He saw me and gave Dad a look. Dad said, "You think I'd let anything happen to her?" Rico let us in. We didn't even have to wait in line.

Dad smiled as he ordered me a wine spritzer, "Light on the wine." Then he put a hand up to the bartender to wait and turned to me. "Red or white?"

"Red."

I drank the pink fizzy water that tasted vaguely of blood and watched couples swirl around me. It was not the mindless flesh-press of a regular American nightclub, nor did it resemble the lopsided lust buffet of the strip club I would work in when I was eighteen—and it was worlds away from the unhip, nun-censored gyrations of the Saint Francis of Assisi parish hall. It was a salsa club. Salsa dancing took skill and grace.

"You can dance if you want; I'll be right here." Dad held up his Corona.

I knew, in a theoretical, kitchen-radio-tuned-to-*Caliente-145.7*, dancing-with-my-cousins-at-Aunt-Marisella's-wedding kind of way how to dance to this kind of music. Mom was Colombian; Dad was Argentine—dancing people—and we lived in Miami, after all. But I hadn't conquered Andrew O'Brien and "The Electric Slide." Maybe Dad would let me get drunk instead? I beckoned the bartender.

Dad ordered me a Coke. "It's best to start slow, Lexie."

Halfway through my Coke, a man asked me to dance. Dad pulled him aside and whispered something to him in Spanish. The man nodded and started to walk away. Dad pulled him back and whispered something else. The man smiled and put his hand out to me.

He looked old to me, though he was probably only twenty-one. His name was Arturo. He was short and unhandsome—his nose too beefy for his fine-boned face—but he smelled good, like chocolate and talcum powder. He kept his torso a respectful distance from mine and was very patient in leading me through the steps. We were always less than fifteen feet from Dad who switched to Coke after two Coronas and who cut in every third song to ask if I was having fun.

"Can we do this every Friday?" I asked at midnight when we got back in the car to go home, still leaning into the darkness, still breathing in the boiled-shrimp smell of Biscayne Bay.

"Your mother would kill me."

"Where does she think we were?"

He smiled his bearish smile and patted my hand.

"I told her we were going bowling."

***

I didn't curse him out. Dad kept looking at me in Trappers—his brown eyes huge and divided behind his trifocals—like he expected me to blast him any minute. Why did he have to be so pathetic?

We went back to his apartment in Rutherford.

"I need pictures of you—of us," he said, setting up his tripod.

We sat on his beat-up black leather couch. Flash-pop. Flash-pop. Tom uploaded them for Dad on Dad's computer. I looked like any other kidnap victim in any other proof-of-life photo.

He showed us—well, me really since Tom had been there before—around his apartment. "You and Julian could stay here, Lexie, for a visit. If you want. It's a two-bedroom."

The place was shabby but dark-corner clean, and I was sure Dad's obsession for order meant that a visit from a messy three-year-old (even if I could get Jeff to agree to such a trip—and I couldn't) would send Dad over the edge.

"It sure is clean, Dad. Some things never change, huh?"

***

"I guess it's from when I was a kid. Your grandmother would come home from work and go around the house with a white glove to check for dirt. She beat the hell out of Berta and me if she found any."

He really *was* dying. Dad never spoke about his mother. His father passed away when he was nine—he said his father was nice, worked a lot, and was very sick for a year before he died. His mother died a few months before Tom and I were born, Aunt Berta still lived somewhere in Argentina, and all Mom would ever say about Dad's mother was that she was 'a difficult person.' Mom's euphemisms tended towards the opaque—her hair could be on fire, and she'd say she was feeling 'warm around the ears'— but as a child, I believed everything she said.

Would I talk about such things with Julian someday when I was dying? Would I tell my son his grandfather took all the money in my bank account (more than a thousand dollars) the week before my eighteenth birthday? That I didn't find out until months later when I needed that money to pay for school? That my father had applied for credit cards in my name, maxed them out, and not paid the bills? That I'd had to change my social security number when I was twenty-one—like a criminal or a battered wife—to feel safe from him?

For these and other reasons, I'd nicknamed my father The Evil Vortex of Doom. I came in from Christmas shopping one Christmas Eve a few years back, and Jeff asked, "Do you want to know if The Evil Vortex of Doom calls, or do you want me to erase the message?" Dad always called on my birthday and holidays and left a weepy message saying he missed me and loved me.

Was it my grandmother's fault? Was some part of her always beating some part of Dad? What else had she done to him?

"I'm sorry that happened to you, Dad."

Tom and Dad looked at me, surprised. They'd expected me to say, 'served you right'?

***

Dad offered to drive me to LaGuardia at the end of my week with Tom. He picked me up early. His shaking made me nervous. I asked, "Mind if I drive?" Wearing his old, good-dad smile, he said, "Whatever makes you happy, Princess," and handed me the keys. We had pizza at Gino's in Queens. We swung by Damiano's; he bought me a slice of cheesecake to take on the plane.

I sent him a Father's Day card and some pictures of Julian.

***

Three months before Dad had his final heart attack, I'd taken to calling him on my way home from counseling. Tom had up and moved to Cartagena for good (lots of nightclubs to work and nineteen cousins, so no shortage of cheap places to live) which meant calling him from my cell phone during the day was out of the question. Mom worked two jobs. I only ever caught her on her day off. So, I called Dad. He always answered the phone. He always made time to talk. There's a lot to be said for that.

Eventually, (on the advice of my counselor) I felt brave enough to ask Dad about some of the things I'd wondered about my whole life. One day I said, "I'm curious about your mom."

"Let's talk about books, Lexie," he said. "I know how you love books."

"Okay." Not okay. Didn't he owe me this? "Well, tell me about Argentina, then."

He was born in Buenos Aires and lived there until he was fourteen. These were things I knew.

"It's been so long. I don't remember."

I felt my goodwill slipping. "Tell me something, Dad. Anything."

I was stuck in traffic behind a black van with a bumper sticker that read: I'm forgiven. Are you?

Dad said, "My father never knew his father—never even saw a picture of him. He caught my grandmother in bed with another man when she was pregnant with my father, and he left. That's the story. I don't know if it's true. But my father grew up without a father. He was a twin—like you—but his brother died when he was still a baby."

"Oh my God."

That night I would make Tom promise not to ever die.

"I'm only telling you this because you asked." His smoker's cough rustled with sadness. "Your grandmother, my mom, was—I hate to say this—a promiscuous woman. When Berta and I were young kids." He coughed. "When my dad, your grandfather, was still alive—she would take us to this apartment by the train tracks, and we'd hear her moaning in there with some man."

"You don't have to tell me anymore, Dad. It's okay. I mean, it's horrible, but you don't have to say more."

"Sometimes," he went on, "we were there for a long time. We

were bored. Berta did homework, and she knew how loud she could put on the radio without getting in trouble—so we listened to music when she was done. We danced. It was fun. But we were too loud once and got in trouble. Berta stuck to her homework after that. I wasn't such a good student, so I cleaned: floors, cabinets, pots and pans, shoes. It was the only thing that didn't get me in trouble. Sometimes, if I polished the man's shoes, he'd give me a caramel when they came out."

Traffic was stopped. A homeless man tapped on my window. I gave him a dollar. I'd never done that before.

Dad's breathing was terrible in my ear. He said, "She said my dad ran around on her, too. I never saw that. Maybe he did. I only remember him one time really well from before he got sick."

Traffic started moving again. I was almost home.

"Yeah, Dad?"

He was talking now. "There was a church carnival in the park near where we lived. My father bought a chance in the raffle and won. He said that since I'd picked the winning ticket, I could have half the pot. It was, like, five U.S. dollars—but to me, it felt like a million. I bought *alfajores* for him and me, a record for Berta, and one of those little bars of soap shaped like a rose for my mother. When we came home with presents that day, it was the only time everyone was happy at the same time." He coughed. A lot. Then stopped. "Then my father got very sick."

"How did your dad die?" My grandfather was thirty-three when he died. I'd always wondered how.

"Tuberculosis." Dad's cough was wet this time. "I wish you'd come to see me, Lexie. I miss you, and I'm dying to meet Julian." Dad always sounded happy when he said Julian's name.

I would get Julian from his grandparents in an hour. We'd

stop for Chinese food and eat chicken chow fun out of the box. Julian would get sauce all over himself. I'd wet a napkin and clean his beautiful face. He'd protest, giggling that it tickled. I'd make a mental note to tell my counselor I'd thought up another reason to live.

"I have a job interview on Thursday, Dad. If I get the job, we'll be able to visit. I promise."

I was home. Same beige suburban driveway. Same electric garage door grinding open. Jeff's hand saw and hedge clippers, which he'd left behind, hanging tidily from hooks on the raw wood of the wall inside; Julian's red tricycle parked in the corner. A "For Sale" sign swinging from chains on a post in the yard.

"I heard the garage door, Lexie. I'll let you go, my Princess. There are dishes in the sink. I love you. Kiss Julian for me."

"Okay, bye, Dad. Love you, too. Take care."

We spoke two more times before Tom called me to say Dad had died. We went to Rutherford to get his ashes and a few mementos. He'd kept the Father's Day card I sent him—the receipts from Gino's and Damiano's tucked in among the photos of me and Julian. His bed was perfectly made. There were no dishes in the sink.

Cream

The waiter leaned his handsome head over the booth in response to Gwen's beckoning look—a look that was all Gwen had ever needed to do to summon a man.

This dimple-smiled man smelled like French toast. Maybe.

The whole room smelled like French toast.

His smile licked at Gwen's vulnerabilities.

"What do you need?" he asked.

Her marriage counselor had asked the same question.

Gwen needed to ask herself *Is this the right decision for my marriage?* instead of *Will this make a good story?* and behave accordingly.

But the month-long writers' retreat had left her feeling touch-deprived.

And the waiter was close enough to touch.

"Cream," Gwen said—and touched his chin quickly with her right index finger. He had that trendy five-day stubble every man under fifty was wearing these days. His was softer than she expected.

His smile didn't falter, but his eyes widened.

"Is half and half okay?"

If only it were.

But Gwen understood that marriage was all or nothing.

"Half and half—yes. Thank you."

He left.

Lana returned to the table.

"I touched his chin," Gwen muttered.

"You what?"

"I touched his chin. The waiter's chin. Just for a second. Not even a second."

"Hmm." Lana swirled a poached egg into her grits.

Gwen picked up a strip of bacon and held it without taking a bite.

"Am I a creepy old woman?"

"Nah." Lana speared a piece of pineapple into her mouth.

"How old do you think he is?"

Lana glanced at the waiter who was taking orders a few tables away. "Twenty-seven?"

They pondered the number in middle-aged silence.

"I thought he looked twenty-eight."

"Okay."

Gwen spooned honey onto her oatmeal. "Which still makes him ten years younger than me."

"Did he mind?"

Gwen tried not to assume every man she met wanted to have sex with her—but she'd learned, with some difficulty, that there was a world of difference between assumptions and reality.

"I don't think so—but maybe he's polite. Maybe he's just a good waiter angling for a tip... I crossed a line, Lana—Jesus, how creepy! Imagine if I were a man and he was a girl!"

"I think the double standard works in your favor here, Gwen."

Gwen regarded her plate, uncertain now, of her appetite.

"I'm gonna apologize."

Lana put down her fork. "Seriously?"

"I don't know."

Lana picked up her fork and attacked her food.

Gwen pushed aside the bacon and eggs and ate her oatmeal slowly. It was the steel-cut kind: creamy and satisfying. Unlike bacon and eggs, it would not harden her arteries. She was old enough now to care about the consequences to her heart.

The waiter arrived with Gwen's cream.

"Can I get you anything else?"

Lana's phone rang, and she excused herself from the table. The waiter stayed.

"I'm sorry," Gwen said.

"No problem."

"No, I mean, I'm sorry I touched your chin before."

This was not altogether true, but it was the right thing to say.

"You're good."

Was she? She'd spent the entire retreat avoiding adultery—and had succeeded in the face of sensual poets, wry novelists, and very sexy, very direct journalists. That was good, wasn't it?

"No, I mean, I thought about it, and if I were a man and you were a woman it would be, well, kinda criminal—"

"I don't mind."

He smiled at Gwen in a way now that made her blush—a way that made her pat her scruples to check that they hadn't melted. She would not fail on her last day in town—and most certainly not with a waiter pouring coffee at a brunch buffet—no matter how tall, dazzling, and sweet-smiled he was.

"Can I ask you something?" Gwen said, tilting her head, inviting him closer.

He inclined his body toward her. "Sure."

"How old are you?"

"Twenty-four."

Gwen winced.

"Why?"

"I thought you were a little older."

"Nope, must be the beard." He touched his cheek. "I'm still a child."

(More of his swelter-inducing smile.)

"If I weren't a happily married woman, I'd make all kinds of indecent proposals to you."

The waiter straightened up, then stepped a bit closer and offered Gwen his hand to shake. "I'm Patrick, by the way."

"Gwen."

"Nice to meet you."

It felt great, his hand: warm, smooth, firm.

They shook hands for a long time, deaf to the din around them; neither of them let go.

Gwen held his hand in both of hers.

"Are you from here?" he asked.

"No."

"How long are you staying?"

"I leave tonight."

Lana returned to the table.

"I gotta go. Anna's having an issue checking out. I gotta hurry." She dropped an appropriate amount of cash on the table. "She's worried she'll miss her flight."

Lana left.

"This is hard," Patrick said, still holding Gwen's hand. "I have a girlfriend."

"I understand. I'm married, remember?"

Gwen's smile failed. Patrick's, too.

"I've been with her three years," he said. "It's a lot of work."

"I know."

She and Matt had been seeing a marriage counselor for over a year. They could talk to each other again—disagree without resorting to war. Gwen no longer wept in the shower each night, wondering how they'd share the kids without destroying everyone's lives.

"How long you been married?"

My entire adult life, Gwen thought but didn't say. "Eighteen years."

Patrick's eyes widened slightly. He did not say she was older than he'd thought.

"So..." he said.

The baby at the next table let out a lusty, operatic scream.

"I'm happily married like I said..." Gwen released Patrick's hand. "But I'm not sorry I touched your chin."

He laughed, rubbing his chin where she'd touched it.

"Me neither."

He left to wait on other tables.

Gwen finished her coffee, added her cash to Lana's, and headed toward the door.

She knew these opportunities would diminish as she got older. They hadn't yet, but they would. And she wondered, as she often did if making the right decision had robbed her of a good story.

She glanced over her shoulder one last time before pushing the door into the fresh, virtuous air of this unfamiliar city. She found him looking at her, a platter in one hand, waving with the other.

Don't Write About Me

She'd stopped counting after seven paper cuts.

Billing needed to go out by the end of the day. Katie had spent her morning folding hundreds of invoices and stuffing them into envelopes so that recipients' addresses showed in the plastic pane. While she stuffed, she mostly daydreamed about the piece that would be published the following week and the gushing things the editor had said about her work.

Only the paper cuts jerked her back into the moment. Occasionally an invoice wouldn't slide all the way in, the address wouldn't show, and Katie would have to refold and re-stuff—scoring tiny bloodless slices into her un-calloused fingers that would sting each time she washed her hands.

Then the light bulb above her desk burnt out.

There was no ladder in the office—and even if there had been, Katie was not getting on a ladder in high heels or stocking feet. Her ancient desk may have been sturdy enough to hold her, but she wouldn't have bet on it. Her office, a former filing closet, had no windows and no other source of light. She considered dragging a floor lamp in, but when she found the only spare floor lamp, it was broken.

She sighed. The boss liked it dark.

She could work in his office while he was in court, but she hated the stale coffee and sour milk smell of his desk. Also, he'd come back from court eventually, even if it was tomorrow, and she'd need to work at her desk.

What would the boss do if he came back from court to find Katie benighted? He would call his son: the handy one, the one with a ladder—the lawyer who was happier building decks.

She had no wish to see the junior partner of the firm (who'd taken to working from home after the birth of his sixth child). They had a nanny, but he and his wife worked from their home office anyway.

Their absence had given dominion to the dilapidation of the office that had once only crouched in the corners.

It had also given Katie a break from A.J.'s unwanted suggestions—though not entirely. He was still IT. He was still the handyman. He still came by to say hello.

If Katie had not been a cynical woman when she took this job, she was now.

Katie stuffed her reservations down and texted the boss' son: "The light above my desk went out. Not sure what kind of bulb it takes. And we don't have a ladder. And you could probably change it sitting down." A joke and a bit of flattery, because A.J. was tall—basketball tall—and leveraged his size whenever possible.

Had Katie used her charm throughout her life to gain the cooperation of men around her? Yes. Did that make her calculating? Yes. Only Katie had done the math and figured that even factoring in the advantages of long legs and eyelashes, she had still come out behind most of the men she knew. Take A.J., for example. He was smart, but not smarter than Katie. And where Katie hadn't known a lazy day in all her working life, A.J. was indolent: did things when he wanted, if he wanted. The consequences got winded and collapsed before reaching him. A junior partner in his father's law firm. She could see the silver spoon sticking out of his mouth. So, what if she slung an occasional double entendre to get the heavy lifting done?

She never took it very far. She didn't have to. Katie was beautiful in a way that made glib men stammer—a dark, South American beauty seldom seen in the outer exurbs of Chicago. A wink. A smile. An appeal to masculine pride— "Could I borrow your upper body strength?"—almost always won her the cooperation she needed.

She drew double solid yellow lines well. Gracefully. "I'm married—so I'll just have to use my imagination... But thank you for the offer. Made my day."

Working with A.J. every day had been tough, though.

She'd found him physically attractive at first. She'd found herself flirting with him a bit harder than necessary.

But to be fair—in playground parlance—he started it. And she went along with it.

At first.

But Katie was married. Wanted to stay married. Had found the best man in the world and been wise enough and pretty enough to capture him. And Jason didn't care if she flirted. As long as she kept within their lane.

Katie had drawn the lines.

A.J. liked to trace them. With his fingers.

It had gotten to the point where it made her nervous. Decent men took "no" for an answer.

So now she had to maneuver around not decent.

And now she needed him.

He arrived, as he always did, in a mushroom cloud of cologne.

He'd brought no ladder.

"I need to stop at the store to get the right bulb, so I thought I'd see what I need and pick up my ladder on the way back here."

Katie led him into her office.

He closed the door.

The room was completely dark.

She heard the leather slap and metal clink of A.J.'s belt coming undone. A zipper. His breathing.

Katie moved toward the door to leave, but his body was in front of it, blocking it. A second door.

He'd never gone this far before. He'd chased her around, pulled her onto his lap, grabbed her butt—that kind of thing. But nothing like this.

A surge of fear held her breath.

He pinned her left hand behind her back and grabbed her right hand with his left. "I've got your ladder right here," he said, and put her right hand around his erect penis and began jerking off.

She tried to break his grip. She could not break his grip.

Every paper cut felt like a stab wound.

"Stop!" She said, in the commanding voice she'd once reserved for badly behaved students.

"That's not why I asked you here!" She said this in case he was confused and because Sun Tzu said to always let your opponent save face.

He released her. Opened the door.

"Are you mad?" he asked, tucking his shirt, zipping his fly.

The door was open, but he was still blocking it.

Knowing her words were all that stood between her and a very large, very strong man who had just proven how little he cared about hurting her, she chose them carefully.

"I'm extremely uncomfortable right now," she said.

He let her pass.

But he followed her, grabbing at her hand even more.

"What do you get out of this?" she asked, reclaiming her hand, wondering if she could snap him out of whatever was motivating this.

"What do you get out of this?" he asked like it was a game.

"Right now?" she asked, with a nonchalance she did not feel, "Kind of a headache."

She walked to his dad's office where there was light and more room.

She should have left.

But he would have followed her. He was parked next to her— he always parked next to her. It frightened her less to be in the office with him than somewhere else where no one would think to look for her.

He shut the door to his dad's office, locked it, and unbuckled his pants again. Grabbed her hand again. Started jerking off again.

Her fear deepened. He could in no way be confused as to her lack of consent.

The bells on the front door jingled.

The boss was back from court.

A.J. released her, zipped, and buckled quickly. Unlocked the door. Click.

That was over. For now.

"What are you guys doing in here?" Big Arnold asked, wheeling his briefcase in behind him.

"I came by to change the light bulb in Katie's office. She was working in yours because hers is a tomb."

"Go change it then."

"Katie, honey, can you go get me a cup of coffee?"

"Of course," Katie said, trembling, trying not to look like she was trembling.

She went to the kitchen and washed her hands—gasping at the pain of a thousand paper cuts.

A long time passed before she stopped shaking.

What could she do?

She could not tell Jason.

He'd insist she quit. And if she refused? Might he not question the truth of her story? After all, Jason earned enough that Katie did not *need* to work. He might not understand why she would choose to stay at Mauvais & Mauvais, LLC. Jason, for all that he loved her, had never lost a job; never suffered long-term unemployment; never, in his adult life, depended upon someone else for money. How could a person who'd never lived without them understand that it might be worse to lose her self-respect and independence than to keep a bad job she wasn't ready to give up? And not on someone else's say so. Why should she complicate her marriage because A.J. was a criminal?

She couldn't tell Big Arnold.

She didn't know for sure that he would take A.J.'s side, but she didn't like her odds. There existed plenty of friction between Big Arnold and A.J. About money. About how much A.J.'s wife loathed Big Arnold—and vice versa. But when things went especially wrong or right, he always called A.J. first. Why should she risk losing her first full-time job in three years job because A.J. was a criminal?

She couldn't go to the cops.

A.J. had grown up with the cops in this small town—and still played basketball with them. Katie remembered a time she had inadvertently dialed 911 at the office, and how A.J. called sixty-two seconds later to ask what was wrong and to tell her which of his teammates was en route.

Also on his team, the County Prosecutor.

Her word against his.

Who was she? A writer with very few publications to her name. An outsider who'd lost her job teaching high school English because a series of nude photos she'd posed for in college (because she was broke and the job had paid well) had surfaced on the Internet fifteen years after they were taken.

She was sure the only reason Big Arnold had hired her was that he was too old to Google anything. Or else he'd found the photos and liked them.

She knew A.J. had seen them.

Her word against his.

But she couldn't live in fear. And right now, she feared him.

She made coffee and filed papers and sent emails and thought for days. Katie was a girl Friday with a master's degree. She had plenty of time to think.

She consulted her best friend who raged for half an hour then guilted her about not calling the police. "Seriously, Katie! How can you not report him? He'll just go out and do this to someone else!"

Now it was on Katie to protect hypothetical women from a crime she didn't commit?

Katie crumpled up inside.

She pictured her life filtered through A.J.'s mind, paraded before the cops and the court.

He could hurt her far more than she could hurt him.

She chatted anonymously online with an attorney in another state.

"Have you told your boss about this?" he asked.

"No."

"Without reporting to your boss, it weakens your case. The law contemplates an effort to report," he said.

"The boss is his dad," she said.

"You should find another job," said the attorney in another state.

Find another job? As though they handed them out on the street like playbills. This was the first job she'd ever had as a legal secretary. And, except for stuffing envelopes and fetching coffee, she didn't hate the work. The clients and cases stoked her imagination. The hours were reasonable. She could feel herself getting better at the things Big Arnold needed besides hot coffee. She could see herself taking on more responsibility in a year. But she had less than a year's experience. All the ads said, 'minimum three years' experience.' And what kind of reference could she expect under the circumstances? She'd planned to work with Big Arnold until he retired—or until someone offered her a better job. People don't hire strangers. But lawyers were, as a rule, rapacious. She knew if she stayed long enough and polished her skills, someone with a broader budget and a less criminally-inclined partner would notice—and, hopefully, poach her.

What *could* she do?

Katie could write. It was one thing she knew for sure she did well. After three months of dictating them to her, Big Arnold let her write all his cease-and-desist letters because, as he put it, "I'm not sure why—but you write scarier letters than I do, Sweetheart." And then he'd laugh like it was terribly funny.

She would write to A.J. At the very least she'd start a paper trail. She could not undo the past, but she would not let him dictate her future.

Katie texted A.J.:

A.J.,

Last Wednesday made me uncomfortable and disappointed—but let me explain:

Re: Disappointed

I'm a flirt. That's just my personality. Now, I admit that I flirt a bit harder with you because you're attractive and you don't object. But when I text you for help at the office I'm not asking for "help." I'm asking for help.

So when you came by last Wednesday and I didn't have the light bulbs, I can see how that could seem disingenuous.

Not the case, A.J. Not the case.

I want to be able to flirt with you and enjoy the fantasy of adultery without doing any actual adultery. I want to brush against you in the hallway, play footsie under the table at parties, and stand too close when we talk. That kind of thing. Not the kind of thing you grabbed me for on Wednesday.

Wednesday tarnished the fantasy. If I wanted that from you, I wouldn't ask you to change a light bulb. I'd be completely unambiguous.

In no fantasy am I ever forced into anything.

Re: Uncomfortable

So when you grabbed my hand, despite my protests and my efforts to pull away—A.J. you are very physically powerful. I could not have pulled myself out of your grip—it reminded me of a bad time when I was a little girl with an uncle who liked to overpower me in a similar way.

Prayer for Relief:

A. Don't do anything like that again and we don't need to mention this again.

B. Just text me back "motion granted" and it's back to a life of smiles.

***

Two days later, to Katie's surprise, he wrote back, "Yes, deal."

She exhaled for the first time in a week.

He could not do it again. She had proof. His own admission. She took screenshots and secreted them away in several safe places.

She had enough breath to whoop when her essay was published the following day—a memoir piece called "Let Me Tell You About the Bad Men I Have Kissed" in which she described, in full-freckled detail, the teachers who'd seduced her in high school.

It wasn't a piece she could send to her mother, but it was published. And that was real. It didn't matter if anyone read it or not. Though, of course, she wanted people to read it.

A few days later, A.J. came by the office.

Katie hadn't expected to see him again so soon—or maybe ever.

He came straight to her office and closed the door.

She did not look up. Did not stop typing.

"I came to apologize."

Katie looked up, though she kept typing.

"Okay."

Click-clack-click-clack-click-clack-click

"I'm sorry about last week."

Katie sighed the sigh of a weary teacher instructing a slow-witted child.

"I told you, we don't have to talk about it ever again."

"I just thought—"

"I'm swamped, A.J. Thank you for apologizing. I gotta finish this letter."

Click-clack-click-clack-click-clack-click

"Sure. Right."

"Goodbye."

He turned to go. Was halfway out the door. Said over his shoulder: "Don't write about me."

Click-clack-click-clack-click-clack-click

"Mmm?" Katie hummed with a nonchalance she did not feel.

He doubled back and stood facing her, sporting his usual boyish dimples.

"Don't write about me in your stories," he repeated. His grin went flaccid. "Because the ladies—they read that shit."

Katie smiled. "Don't worry, A.J., I won't use your real name."

Dreaming of the Netherlands

I noticed her heel-click-hip-twist hourglass silhouette as we walked toward a bright light at the end of a long corridor between Terminal B and Terminal C. My husband, teenaged son, and all the other travelers flowed past on the electric walkway; she and I were the only ones who'd chosen to move on our own locomotion. She clicked along a good twenty feet ahead of me, blonde hair in a chignon, a few locks flying loose around her face. She trod with a long-stride purpose, but her heels could not outpace my flats. I caught up, though I did not overtake her. That's when I noticed the zipper pull on the back of her uniform: a little silver plane-shaped pendant hanging three or four inches from the top of the zipper on a blue-jeweled chain.

"Did the dress come that way?" I asked.

"No," she said.

"I like it."

"Thanks," she said. She smiled with dimples.

I blushed.

The winged pin on her chest—which I'd hoped would say her name—said "The Netherlands".

I'd never been. There were so many places I *had* been... but not there.

I slowed my stride to match hers. She noticed me noticing.

"You should come," she said.

We both walked more slowly. She brushed the inside of my palm with her fingertips.

"I should," I said, blushing harder.

My men hailed me from the end of the hall like a pair of foregone conclusions. I hurried to rejoin them.

I didn't know then we'd be on the same flight where she would serve me water and champagne, coq au vin, strawberry tarts, honeydew like a plate of crescent moons, and an omelet and rose-petal tea; where my men would sleep, one row up, snoring, farting, oblivious; where I'd spend the eight and a half hours between Paris and Boston awake, dreaming of pulling her zipper; where she would offer, in the dark, on her break, somewhere over the Atlantic, to 'tuck me in'; and where I would, foolishly, decline.

The Baby Monitor

Ping. Was it her phone—or a fretful dream?

When the salesman had ticked off all the things the baby monitor could do, Alyssa had asked if it also cooked breakfast and spoke with the dead. "Well," he'd said with a laugh, "it *is* totally HD—and the manufacturer *has* said some of the coolest features haven't been enabled yet."

Ping. Dream.

It was a pricey item, the one thing no one had gifted her from her baby shower registry. Alyssa, who had publicly scoffed at the minute ways a baby monitor monitored a baby, felt secretly reassured. So many people she'd loved had died or left. Archie was her only family now. And even though he was, according to his pediatrician, "a perfectly healthy baby," she carried a constant panic, like her heart had been replaced with a ticking bomb, that he, too, would be taken from her. So, she'd set up the monitor and enabled every notification. She had not imagined how often it would notify her, even though Archie was swaddled and hardly moved when he slept. She was okay with the hyper-vigilance. She'd come to regard the egg-shaped device with its red-beaming camera as her third eye—the only one that never closed. It let her view the entire nursery, take pictures, record videos, listen and speak to the baby, and play lullabies. Plus, it alerted her to noises in the room, changes in Archie's sleeping position, breathing, heart rate, and temperature with a text.

Ping. Phone. Alyssa, dull with sleep, opened the app, and

checked the camera.

A man was standing over Archie's crib, covering the baby's mouth, and holding his nostrils closed.

***

"Call 911." Her father hissed. They'd driven into a tree. "No one can see us from the road. It's too dark."

She had some bruises, maybe a broken arm—her left arm hurt when she tried to move it—but so what? She was right-handed, and pain didn't bother her if she could see an end to it. A broken arm was nothing serious.

Her father hadn't moved since the car stopped. "Call someone, Alyssa. Please."

He was bad off if he was saying please.

She listened in the dark. She heard no people or cars.

His breathing sounded like when you stuck a pin into a sagging foil balloon.

***

Alyssa ran to the baby's room. When she looked around, all she saw was Archie, flailing silently in his crib. She could only see the man when she looked at the monitor's feed on her phone.

He was not a stranger.

"Get away from my baby!" she screamed

He took his hands off the baby, smiled, and vanished.

Had she imagined him?

She still had nightmares about her father. He had always attacked her at night, waiting as long as it took for her to nod off, as though puncturing her sleep was integral to his pleasure. Alyssa didn't remember sleeping as a child—only waiting and dreading.

She had nightmares about everything now, though. They

had started in the six months since Tim had died. When she thought about it, the three years she'd slept with her head on her husband's chest was the only time in her life she hadn't suffered nightmares each time she closed her eyes to sleep. And, consequently, the only time in her life she'd felt truly awake with her eyes open. Only rested people got to feel awake; everyone else simply struggled with consciousness. Tim had protected her from everyone, from everything, from herself, even her dreams. Lately, all her nightmares were of the police officers' knock on her door and identifying Tim at the morgue.

And now, this.

She checked her phone again. No, this was not a dream. There were notifications on her phone. Alyssa had never had a dream that sent text notifications.

That night, she lay awake on a mattress she dragged into the baby's room, her heart a metronome of fear, staring into the monitor's camera feed on her phone. She would stay next to Archie every night for the rest of her life if she could.

Only she knew she couldn't.

She had learned from her foster mother how to be a practical woman. When Alyssa went to her with a problem, Ruth would say, "Ask yourself: What can I do in the next five minutes to make the situation better? Then do it. Keep asking and doing until things get better."

Alyssa could not stitch her eyelids open and stare at her phone every minute for the rest of her life. Tim was gone. Alyssa had no family—save a few far-flung, moribund aunts who did not remember their own names, let alone hers. Tim was gone. She lost touch with her foster parents, Peter and Ruth, physicians, and purposeful Christians when they moved to Sierra Leone to work with Doctors Without Borders after Alyssa graduated college. She missed them immeasurably. Tim was gone. She had no close friends. The only baby shower anyone hosted for her had been by the Holiday and Events Committee at work. They celebrated anyone who paid dues. Alyssa paid dues. Tim was gone. He'd been looking into life insurance—was going to buy some before the baby was born; he promised. And he would have. But he had died first. Alyssa had a good job as a manufacturing systems analyst that she hated. And needed. And a million dollars' life insurance premiums to pay. She would have to go to work.

What could she tell the sitter that wouldn't sound completely insane?

"Don't leave the baby alone, even for a minute. Please, Detta."

"Okay," said Detta, smiling. "Don't worry."

"Not even to answer the door."

"Okay," said Detta. "You look tired, Miss Alyssa."

"Not even to go to the bathroom."

"Are you okay, Miss?" Detta asked, her smile replaced with knit brows.

"Please, Detta. Just promise. Not even for a minute."

"What about when he sleeps, Miss?"

"Especially when he sleeps."

"That will be hard, Miss."

"But you'll do it?"

"Yes, Miss."

Alyssa knew Detta would keep her word.

Even so, after three days, Detta said, "I watch him and watch him, Miss. He's very healthy. Your house is very safe. All he does is normal baby boy things. I think it is not normal to watch a baby so much."

"I'm sorry, Detta."

"What is your worry? I have watched lots of babies. Maybe I can help you. You only have this one. Nothing to compare with. Please, Miss, what is your worry?"

Alyssa hadn't slept in days. At work, she pretended to work and checked the baby monitor app and nanny cams. She knew Detta had toted the baby everywhere, as promised—even sat in the chair beside his crib and read e-books or listened to music while he slept. She didn't have cameras in the bathroom, but there was one facing the bathroom door, and she saw Detta take him in and set him in the empty tub before she closed the door to use the bathroom.

She tumbled around in her thoughts for how to answer Detta's question and said, "You are the best nanny ever. But I can't talk about it. I just can't."

"Miss," Detta began; then stopped. "Miss," she began again, "I cannot keep doing it how you ask. It does not make sense to watch a healthy baby when he's asleep. He will grow up afraid, feeling spied on. Or spoiled, like a king."

"Please, Detta. Just do it a few more days. I'll think of something."

Detta sighed. "Okay, Miss Alyssa. A few more days. But that is all. I am honest. You can replace me if you want. But you know no one will be honest and love Baby Archie as I do."

***

Alyssa couldn't help it: after being awake for three days and nights, she fell asleep.

Ping! Ping! Ping!

She woke up.

Again, she could not see the man when she looked around the room, only through the app. And again, he had his hands covering the baby's nose and mouth.

Archie's arms and legs flailed.

"Stop! Leave him alone!" she shouted through the app.

Again, the man smirked, took his hands off the child, and left.

Alyssa had looked closely at him on the small screen this time. Same argyle sweater over a checked shirt, same flyaway blond hair, same thick fingers, same close-lipped smile. It was definitely her father.

***

Alyssa could have reached the phone in her father's pocket. She could have walked up to the road and flagged someone down for help. But her future held her back.

She rolled the end of her thin, brown braid between her fingers. The way the hair stuck out in aggregate—stiff, yet pliable—reminded her of a paintbrush. She'd always liked it in school when someone would hand her a paintbrush and palette. They rarely cared what she painted as long as she was quiet. And she was always quiet—trying to disappear. She envied animals that could camouflage themselves to avoid predators. Why couldn't she do that? Just blend into the wallpaper? She always painted herself doing it. It always only looked like she'd painted the pattern of the wallpaper.

"What do you think will happen to you if I die?" her father had asked. His voice sounded like he was choking—like he was drowning.

Alyssa didn't say anything; she just imagined herself changing color to match the seat of the car.

***

This, she knew, was untenable. She needed Archie to be safe.

She needed to sleep. She needed to work. She needed Detta not to quit.

Alyssa knew nothing about ghosts, but she knew plenty about her father. Her father had taught tenth-grade remedial reading—a job he said he liked because the girls "Always come half-dressed hoping for a passing grade," and "No one expects these kids to learn anything, so I can do whatever I want." He would leave Alyssa alone at night when he found "a discreet girl," sometimes for weeks at a time. Alyssa always knew who they were by who came out of her father's classroom after school. Remedial reading students never stayed after school to study. The girls were almost always thin, quiet, sleepy-looking brunettes with long hair and forgettable faces.

Like Alyssa. Had anyone noticed her, she would have been voted "Most Likely to Be Forgotten on the School Bus." There was no penalty for falling asleep on the bus. And she was so sleepy.

But she did all she could not to fall asleep in class or do poorly in any subject. Teachers called home if you failed or fell asleep. If a teacher called home about something bad Alyssa had done, it ensured a beating on top of everything else.

Her grades improved after her father died. She still had nightmares, but she'd stopped having to manage the constant fear. How light she felt after the fear lifted.

How heavy she felt now that it had returned.

Because she feared him, alive or dead. Though now he was, most certainly, dead.

She needed to find out what the old man wanted. He always had a plan—a lesson to teach—just as he'd spent all those years teaching her how to hold her body this way or that to give a man pleasure; and how to show respect for her elders; and how to leave her body to keep from losing her mind.

But she wasn't a helpless child anymore. She would not let him hurt Archie or terrorize her. He'd terrorized her every day for the first fifteen years of her life. Then she'd been free. Free for fifteen years.

She never took her freedom for granted. It felt good to live.

***

An hour or ten minutes or five minutes had passed.

"You can sit there while I bleed to death, Coquette" he wheezed. "But I will never let you go. The bell doesn't dismiss the class. The teacher dismisses the class."

Fifteen-year-old Alyssa shuddered but did not move.

It felt good being where he could not twist her arm.

Parts of a tree had come through the windshield, but only on his side. He could not move. If he could, he would. It was as though he'd been caught under a falling portcullis.

Could she sit there while he died? What if it took too long? She steeled herself. She had gambled, grabbing the wheel, propelling them into the woods off a little-traveled stretch of highway at seventy-five miles per hour late at night.

"Where are we going?" she'd asked him before the crash.

"I'm taking you away. Your health teacher asked me some funny questions at the last conference. I got a job where nobody knows us. And you're done with school."

That was when she grabbed the wheel.

***

Alyssa tried calling him through the app: "Dad! Dad! I know you want to teach me something. Come and school your little Coquette."

He did not appear.

For two days Alyssa called to him through the baby monitor. She was afraid to take Archie anywhere the monitor was not. She didn't even bathe him. There was no Wi-Fi in the bathroom. She worried she'd place him in the tub, and her father would drown him.

***

No one had seen them go off the road.

She wouldn't have cared if she'd died. She believed in the finality of death. No, it made no difference which of them died in the wreck.

And if they both lived? He could make her life no worse. Maybe he'd kill her like he always said he would. That would be a relief.

This was best, though—if she lived and he died.

She closed her eyes and waited.

***

On the third night, she couldn't see him, but she could hear him.

"You called."

Alyssa trembled. She'd counted on the finality of death, yet here he was. She sought her fifteen-year-old self's resolve; like so many things it felt just out of reach. "You can fake courage," her foster dad, Peter, used to say. "No one can tell the difference." She would fake courage.

Alyssa took a deep breath. "What do you want?" she asked.

"Oh," he said, drawing out the syllable, "to spend some time with my grandson. Like other grandpas."

"You're not welcome here."

"I know. I had to let myself in. These modern marvels..." He caressed the baby monitor. "It's so lovely to be able to talk with you again. And I like it here—with you, and young Archie."

"What do you want?"

"I'm lonely."

It was what he'd always whispered in her ear when he woke her. She could hardly breathe, but she had his attention. "You can't resolve a problem with someone unless you have their attention," Ruth had said.

"Go make friends with another ghost, Dad."

"That's what I'm trying to do."

Alyssa did what she could to stanch the rage. He loved to watch her flinch. "You can't have him," she said with forced calm.

"Oh, but I can," he said, winding his fingers around Archie's throat—not squeezing, just winding. "I can take him with me if I want."

She tried to pry his fingers off the baby but couldn't.

Alyssa let out an involuntary scream.

Archie began to wail.

"Calm yourself, Coquette." He grinned into the camera. "You're upsetting my grandson."

Alyssa kept her eyes glued to the screen.

He lifted his hand off the child. Alyssa picked Archie up and soothed him. The way he burrowed into her chest had become her life's purpose.

"You were gone for fifteen years," Alyssa said quietly to no one.

"I never left. I told you I'd never let you go."

"But I was free."

***

She'd waited until he'd stopped breathing for a long time. She didn't know how long, but not as long as she'd feared. It was still night. Still dark.

She crawled out the passenger window, cutting her arms and legs on broken glass. The pain in her arm made her gasp with each movement. She would be covered in blood by the time she scrambled back up to the road. That was okay. He was dead. Her arm would heal. Then she could paint something besides wallpaper.

***

"You weren't free, Coquette. I was just biding my time."

Alyssa held the phone in one hand and cradled Archie in the other.

"I was waiting for a teachable moment, waiting for you to care about something."

"So? What? I didn't care about Tim?"

"So? What? That escaped my notice? Who do you think pushed his bike in front of the truck, Coquette?"

He'd taken Tim? Alyssa sat down quickly in the chair beside the crib to keep from falling. But she didn't scream or cry. She needed to think.

"So why not just take Archie, too?"

"I've thought about it, Coquette. I have."

"And?"

"Things change. Times change." He touched a button on the baby monitor and "Brahm's Lullaby" issued from the speaker. "There's my legacy to consider. He's a nice healthy boy. Could carry on my bloodline."

"He is, Dad. A nice healthy boy. I'll change his name to yours if you want. Tell him nice things about you. I can lie. You taught me how to lie well." She paused. "Spare him."

Her father laughed. "But I can't just let you get away with killing me, Coquette. What kind of father would I be—sparing the rod? Where's the lesson in that?"

"Taking Tim was enough." Where was Tim's ghost? Wouldn't Tim's ghost be able to stop her father? "Do you ever see Tim?"

"Don't you mean *Why the hell isn't he helping his wife and son?*" The old man guffawed. "Tim would help you if he could. But his soul is a lot purer than mine; he was drafted to fight some greater evil.

"Apparently, I'm small beer—"

"You're the greater evil."

"Don't be so selfish."

"Taking Tim was enough."

"No way. You could be happy again, Coquette. You're young. Healthy. With a nice, healthy son."

Archie had stopped crying. Alyssa checked to make sure he was breathing. He was.

"I'll do anything."

"Oh, I know you will. But I'm already dead. You can't kill me this time."

"Anything," she said. Her throat and tongue felt hot and dry.

"Okay."

"Okay, what?"

"Okay, I'll spare the baby."

"Just like that?" Alyssa asked. She was shaking all over.

"But you'll have to do 'anything.'"

"What do I have to do?"

"Leave him behind."

This was, he knew, the worst thing he could ask her to do. Alyssa had grown up without a mother. It was a permanent abyss.

"And go where?" she asked, though she already knew.

"Come with me."

Death on his terms. Of course.

"How do I know you won't harm him?"

"You'll be able to see him on the monitor, same as me."

"You could hurt him while I watched."

"No, no, Coquette. I'll be busy with you. You'll be my little Coquette again. As long as you stay with me, as long as you do what I want—and you know what I want—I won't hurt the boy. I'll be busy. With you. Forever. There's no sleeping once you're dead, Coquette. No sleeping, no eating, no whizzing, no squatting. Just watching the living and spending time with family."

"You mean when he dies, he'll be with us?"

"Depends on him. He could end up with Tim. He might have a family of his own. Maybe a wife that dies first... And, besides, I'll be busy with you forever. I won't seek him out."

"Why wouldn't I end up with Tim instead of you?"

"Your soul isn't that pure, Coquette. You didn't need to kill me. You could've reported me to the authorities. Or run away. I didn't keep you locked in a closet. You had options, Coquette, and you picked murder. You belong with me."

"You belong in hell."

"Don't be scared, Coquette. Hell isn't nearly as hermetic as it used to be. There's Wi-Fi."

Alyssa switched off the baby monitor and her phone.

Archie began to flail.

Alyssa turned the monitor and her phone back on.

"Nice try, Coquette. But you can't put a genie back in its bottle."

"Let go of him!"

He let go, and Archie gasped and screamed.

"I won't let go next time."

Her father had never issued an empty threat.

But Archie's soul was pure! He would surely end up with Tim.

But only if he died.

Archie dying was not an option.

Where the hell was God?

"I'll give you one minute to decide."

Who knew? Maybe hell was temporary, too. Or Tim would come for her. Or she'd find some way that hadn't been invented yet to be with Archie.

Archie dying was not an option.

"I'll go with you," Alyssa said.

This was the last time she would hold him. She'd done one good thing.

She set Archie in his crib.

"I've always wanted to throw a hairdryer in the tub while you bathed."

"That would look like suicide. I can't kill myself. The insurance won't pay if I kill myself."

He paused for a full minute, as though reconsidering their deal.

"Lucky for you, I'm in a good mood," he said, smiling that same close-lipped smile. "I can make it look like natural causes."

He stared at her through the camera. She shivered.

"I've missed you, Coquette."

"He'll be alone. How can I be sure he'll be okay?"

"Tomorrow is Monday. Detta will be here at 7:00. The boy wakes up at 7:30...He'll be fine."

Death Comes to the Office for Daniel Downer

He might've dispatched one of his Angels to do it, but Death knew Daniel would resist, and his best Angel was on vacation, harvesting souls in Costa Rica for the next month, so Death resolved to take Daniel himself.

He'd gone to Daniel's house on Mirror Lake, but Daniel pretended not to be home, so Death—patient in the knowledge that he always wins—decided to catch up with him at the office. He would just call, pretend he needed a lawyer because he'd been in a terrible, disfiguring accident with someone driving for a well-insured major company, and make an appointment.

Death called on a Friday and spoke with one of Daniel's assistants who took down all the details of his 'accident and injuries.' She made 'Mort LeJour' an appointment for Monday at ten.

Death didn't have much going on that weekend, but he was restless, so he went to the nearest nursing home and killed some time harvesting souls he'd put on the back burner years ago. They were, for the most part, happy to see him.

He remained restless, so he visited all the emergency rooms in the area and harvested the souls of some people who looked terrified to find him in their beds. He didn't blame them, but God's orders were God's orders.

That did not cure his restlessness, so he took a train to the city and got off in the roughest neighborhood. He hadn't been to the South Side in years. He remembered when it was an enclave of Polish immigrants and not nearly as rough. He had an Angel— a crazy motherfucker, to be honest with you—who liked harvesting on the South Side. And Death, to be honest with you, had qualms about God's orders concerning the South Side, so he avoided it.

But today he needed to remember that the poor died early, at random, and in droves. He needed to do something to make himself feel better about harvesting Daniel Downer's soul. Daniel Downer was a wealthy, selfish ambulance chaser in his seventies; Death should have been looking forward to it.

He wasn't. His least favorite harvests were people like Daniel who would try anything to get out of it. He just didn't like being in the same room with people who thought they were so special they should be passed over, eternally.

Death carried out God's orders on the South Side and got the hell out of there—back to the suburbs, where harvesting was clean, quiet, and generally appropriate business.

Monday came. Death arrived for his appointment at ten on the dot. He could be punctual when it suited him. And he just wanted to get this over with.

Daniel wasn't there. Something had come up.

The receptionist rescheduled him for the following day at 3:00 p.m.

Death arrived at the appointed time. Daniel was late. Death waited.

Daniel walked in at 3:30, carrying a McDonald's bag and holding a cup of coffee at such an angle that he left a trail of it throughout the office. His hair was wet under his ball cap, and he wore a coffee-spotted T-shirt inside out.

Didn't lawyers dress up for work?

Death remembered when everyone dressed up for work. He shrugged inwardly. People wore flip-flops to church these days. The world had gone to pajamas. Still—inside out?

Daniel ushered Death into his office where he proceeded to eat hotcakes with syrup and eggs—and talk with his mouth full between bites. Bits of egg clung to his unkempt beard.

Death nearly gagged, then said, "I am Death. I have come to harvest your soul on orders from God."

Daniel tried to climb out the nearest window, thinking he could jump down. They were only on the second floor. That was ten feet up, right? He was six feet tall. Surely, he could jump four feet. But he didn't. He got stuck in the window.

Death said, "Make peace with God or whatever. This won't take long."

"But who will take care of my ninety-five-year-old mother if I die?"

Death said, "Your sister."

"She's useless."

Death said, "Fine, I'll take care of your mom for you."

"Forget it. My sister will do okay."

Death said, "I'll probably take care of your mom soon either way."

"I know I shouldn't say this, Mort, but that would be a relief—but are you sure you're here for me? My son and I have the same first and last name. Are you sure you're here for Daniel Downer *Senior*?"

Death paused, then said, "My orders are pretty clear. And they come from—"

Daniel interrupted, "Anyone can make a mistake, Mort."

Death went on as though Daniel hadn't interrupted, "My orders come from God. And I gotta say, Daniel—in all my eternity of doing this job, I have never met anyone who tried to have me take their kid instead. That's..."

Daniel interrupted, "What do you know about my kid? My kid is an ingrate! All my kids are ingrates! I gave them everything! Coached their little league; went to their dance recitals; worked my ass off so they could go to good schools; paid for their colleges. My namesake, the one you might or might not be mistaking me for—"

Death said, "Excuse me—"

"No," Daniel said. "Let me finish! My son, Daniel Downer the Second—which by the way should make me 'the First,' not 'Senior' for Pete's sake I'm not that old—I took him as my business partner right out of law school! Full partner! You know how long he'd have to work to make partner anywhere else? We practiced together for fifteen years, and then he leaves his first wife and three kids after knocking up the bimbo he's married to now, and because she doesn't like me, he left me to practice alone here like some kind of asshole. He stole from me, too! Two hundred thousand dollars! I can't prove it, but one of these days—and on top of everything, Mort, my wife of forty years divorced me. Do you have any idea how devastating that is?! Forty years! And she divorces me! That woman is heartless! Never marry a girl who graduated from Catholic school. She took all my money! I'm broke! Do you hear me? Broke! That's why I'm still working in this shithole at my age!"

Death sat stoically in his chair. It wasn't that he couldn't take Daniel Downer anytime he wanted; it was that he was getting too old for the grappling. And this guy was a grappler. But maybe...

Death said, "With all due respect, Daniel, what do you have to live for?"

Daniel thought for a minute, then said, "Nothing."

Death said, "Then why don't you let me take you out of this pain?"

Daniel said, "You don't get to tell me what to do!"

Death asked, "Does anybody love you?"

"No."

Death asked, "Do you love anybody?"

"My ex-wife."

"I don't believe you."

"No, it's true. I love her."

"You don't even love your kids, Daniel. I'm supposed to believe you love your ex-wife?"

"But I do."

"Prove it."

"How?"

"Tell you what: I can give you a reprieve."

"Yeah?"

"Yeah."

"What do I have to do?"

"Give me her address."

"Why?"

"I'll take her instead."

Daniel, who was still stuck in the window, tried prying the window open wider. It didn't budge. He looked Death in the eye.

"I get a reprieve if I give you her address? For how long?"

Death waited for a beat before replying, "Depends."

"What if I give you the wrong address?"

"I could make it painful for you, Daniel, when I come back. And I would come right back."

"Won't it be painful this time?"

"Maybe."

"You don't know?! Wait! How can you make sure it's painful

next time if you don't know whether it will be painful this time?"

"If you give me the wrong address, I'll know you really love her. So, I'll make sure I find her, and I'll take her, too. You'll know that. And that will be painful."

"You can't do that! You said you take your orders from God! He says who goes!"

"God permits me discretion in these matters."

Daniel jerked himself out the window, onto the cold pavement of a Midwestern winter afternoon. Smacked his head hard on the concrete.

Death left the office relieved. He hated grapplers.

Mayor Daley at the Superdawg ®

Wally Perdu had buried his mother that morning in a lavish ceremony complete with a string quartet and a teak casket lined with real silk, wept real tears while his grown children wrestled fake expressions of grief onto their bored faces, and paid for everything out of the savings his now ex-wife had halved in their recent divorce—his mother's long-hovering death having depleted all her money. They'd left him alone when it was over—work, squirming children, unwavering apathy—and all Wally wanted now was a Superdawg. He hadn't eaten all day—couldn't eat any of the death-flavored food at the funeral home and never had more than a frozen pot pie in the house since Barb moved out two years ago. He couldn't face a frozen pot pie today.

He would go to Superdawg, home of the Superdawg—the only place in the world that hadn't changed since he was a kid. His mouth watered thinking about the pickle, the piccalilli, the hot peppers, and the Spanish onions atop the all-beef dawg—the whole kit embraced by a poppy-seed bun. It would make him feel young again for a little while. It always did.

"You'll live longer if you eat fewer hotdogs, Wally," his doctor had admonished during his yearly physical.

"I'm sixty-eight, Doc," Wally had said, a hand on his expanding paunch. When had he gotten so fat? He'd always been brawny. Now it was like his shoulders had fallen into his stomach. "I'm not as afraid to die as I am of living without hotdogs."

"It's my job to keep you alive and healthy, Wally."

"You can't want it more than I do, Doc."

Wally ordered his Superdawg and waited.

Would his children care if he choked to death on a hotdog? Probably not, but it wouldn't offend him then. For one thing, he'd be dead. He was either going to Heaven where he wouldn't give a damn if they cared or not or Hell where he wouldn't give a damn if they cared or not. For another thing, choking to death on a Superdawg sounded like an excellent way to die. Quick. Reasonably painless. And he'd die doing something he loved.

What else did Wally love?

His children? The ones who owed him hundreds of thousands of dollars? Who only called when they needed a loan they would never repay? He didn't know why he took their calls anymore, other than missing their voices. They didn't take his calls.

If anyone asked, he'd say he loved his grandkids, but that would be a mottled truth. His grandchildren made him sad. They seldom looked up from their electronic worlds, and when they did, they avoided eye contact. He had no talent for bonding with them, just as he'd had no talent for bonding with his children when they were young. He'd been happy enough to watch Barb make them sparkle with her magic for getting kids to roll snowballs and make mud pies. But Barb was not there with Wally now—and so the 'grands', as they'd called them, sniffed at him like a suspect piece of meat and went back to their video games.

Barb. For all that she'd left him after forty years of marriage, he loved her—would take her back if she came knocking.

But it hadn't worked out that way. Instead, Wally found himself driving past her house—sometimes in the middle of the night when he couldn't sleep because she wasn't beside him.

Would he ever sleep again?

They handed him his Superdawg.

What was the point of sleep anyway?

True to his ritual, Wally walked to the car, Superdawg in one hand, a cola, and a bag of fries in the other. It was January, and most people turtled into their coats, but Wally didn't believe in coats. Rarely felt cold. People always said, "You'll freeze to death!" Wally, an actuary for a local life insurance company, knew all the ways and likelihoods of people dying in the city. Without even accounting for age, he knew more than 25,000 people died of heart disease in Chicago the previous year, as compared with fewer than thirty deaths by hypothermia. A broad-shouldered Chicago wind frisked him. As usual, Wally got goosebumps but did not die. He focused on his balance. To drop the food would only deepen his grief.

He'd left the doors unlocked to make this maneuver simpler. He could coax the door open with one finger. For though he felt his body betraying him in ways both big and small the last eight years (bum hip, bum knee, fallen arches from all the running he'd done as a younger man—you can't outrun Death, his body told him, more and more stridently), he still had strong hands— could open a pickle jar without those gizmos they marketed to people his age on infomercials at 3:00 a.m.

He eased into the driver's seat and set his drink in the cupholder. Victorious against Death and the weather, he perched the dawg on his knee and started the car.

Wally pulled out of the parking lot, masticating quietly, focused on the pleasure of the first bite.

Someone coughed in the backseat.

"Who's there?!" Wally had the steering wheel in one hand

and his Superdawg in the other.

"Drive to the bank," said a strange man's voice.

"Get out of my car!"

"I will," said the man who now had both hands around Wally's neck. "But first we're going to your bank to make a withdrawal."

Wally nearly choked on the piece of hotdog he'd been about to swallow before the stranger gripped his throat. This was not what he'd had in mind when he'd imagined choking to death on a Superdawg.

More than 1,500 people had been murdered in Chicago the preceding year. Homicide: *much* more likely than hypothermia.

How many were strangled? The stat was similar to hypothermia. But what a ghastly way to die. Still, only wife-beaters and complete psychopaths strangled someone to death…

"I don't have any money in the bank." His Social Security check hadn't come yet, he'd spent his entire paycheck, and neither the string quartet nor the funeral home would accept credit cards.

"A guy who drives this car has money in the bank."

This stupid car: a Mercedes E-300, bought at the beginning of the end—a nice car because, as she was moving out Barb had accused him of being a 'cheapo,' so he'd gone and bought this stupid car, brand new, paid cash (his long-time banker and friend Gil called him to personally ascertain Wally was compos mentis before approving such an unusually large draft), and drove to his sister-in-law's house (where Barb was living) to show it to her. Barb had laughed a mean kind of laugh he'd never heard before. *That's the problem, Wally. You realize everything too late. You're a step behind. I've always had to tell you what to do and when to do it. I'm tired of it.* She went on, *The kids are*

*grown, my folks are dead, and I don't have to do it anymore.
I'm free. I'm free of you, Wally. I'm taking half and I'm going to
enjoy the rest of my life.*

"This car was a mistake," Wally muttered, slowing down for
a yellow light.

"You can make this light," said the stranger, tightening his
grip.

"Look right." The stranger looked where Wally pointed with
his chin. "That cop might disagree."

He stopped at the light. He probably should have run it; let
the cop pull them over. Only Wally hated cops—feared them.
He'd been beaten up by cops once at the hospital after a nurse he
did not remember threatening had called 9-1-1. The nurse had
refused to let him see his sick mother. He'd probably been out of
line with the nurse—probably had threatened to break her
finger—but he'd never touched her. The cops, though, had
tackled and kneed him, wrenched his arm out of its socket, then
charged him with resisting arrest. He'd been acquitted, but the
fear had not left him. That was three years ago.

"Fine," said the stranger, taking his hands off Wally's throat.
"But don't even think about hopping out."

He had considered hopping out but remembered his hip and
his knee and had zero interest in a physical altercation with the
much younger, much stronger stranger. "I don't hop anymore,
Mister." Wally pointed to his handicapped parking placard.
"And thanks."

"What for?"

"For taking your hands off my throat. I'm starving. And
while I don't especially want to be strangled to death, starving to
death would be more painful."

Wally made a show of taking an enormous bite.

The stranger laughed. He had a good laugh. The laugh of a guy who'd beat you at bowling, then buy you a beer and shoot the shit with you till last call.

Wally laughed, too.

Maybe the stranger wouldn't kill him. Do you kill a guy who makes you laugh? Wally wished he had a formula for the probability of it.

"What do you want more: money or to kill me?"

The stranger answered slowly: "Money, I guess."

"You need money."

"Yeah."

Wally offered his fries. The stranger ate some fries.

"I paid for my mother's funeral this morning. It was expensive. I don't have enough money in my bank account to make it worth it to you to risk being caught on all those bank cameras."

"So what? I'm supposed to take a few fries and let you go?"

This was not a joke, and Wally did not laugh.

"My wife of forty years just divorced me. She took all the money and left me with all the stuff—"

"Boo-hoo," said the stranger.

"I'm not asking for sympathy, Mister. I'm explaining about the money. Here's my wallet. I carry only enough cash for a Superdawg—but you can go to town with my credit card. I'll wait a few hours before canceling it. You can buy some stuff to fence in a few hours."

"Yeah," said the stranger. "Sip of your drink?"

Wally handed him the cup. The stranger slurped loudly.

"And since you want money more than you want to kill me, then why don't I pull over. I can stop at a park or something and finish my hotdog. Here, have my phone. I barely know how to use the damned thing anyway. I'll leave the keys on the seat. I leave the car; you take the car. It's a nice car, right?"

"Yeah."

"So, you don't kill me, and you get a bunch of stuff. Deal?"

"I don't know anyone wants to buy a car."

"I'm just saying, you can have it if you want it."

"I need cash."

"You have my wallet."

The stranger unzipped Wally's wallet.

"There's five bucks in here."

"I have a receipt from the bank with my balance on it from my withdrawal this morning tucked behind my credit card."

"Thirty-three dollars?"

"Like I told you."

The stranger was silent for a minute. Wally glanced with longing at his hotdog.

"What'll you tell the cops?"

"I left my stuff in the car and someone drove off with it."

"They'll ask what I look like."

"I don't know what you look like. I haven't turned around to look at you because I've been driving, and when I've glanced in the rearview all I see is the bill of your cap. You're a guy in a Chicago Bears hat. You could be Mayor Daley for all I know."

The stranger laughed again. "Okay."

"Deal?"

"Deal."

Wally pulled over, took his food, left his keys and phone on the seat, and walked across the street to the icy cemetery. He lowered himself onto the bench beside his mother's grave and finished his hotdog without further incident.

Lap Dance

He told himself he could drink a beer and watch the women—that he didn't really have to touch anyone. He also held fast to the idea that customers weren't allowed to touch the girls in such places; and that the girls probably didn't want to touch the customers very much, anyway, so he'd be safe. Gabe wore thick glasses. His aversion to haircuts showed in the way his black hair hung from his scalp like a neglected pelt. Depending on whether he'd been feeding his depression or starving it, his clothes were either too tight or too loose. And he was shy.

He had not expected the wall of smoke he walked into after paying the five-dollar cover charge—smoking indoors had been banned in Arkansas since 2006—but then, Gabe wasn't there for his health. Between the smoke and the extremely dim lighting, he could barely see. Music engulfed him—music so loud, so vibratory, Gabe felt aware of his appendix. He stood just inside the door for a minute while his eyes adjusted, and his lungs stirred with longing; Gabe hadn't smoked in three years. Surely, they sold cigarettes at Delilah's Cabaret.

When he could see, he looked around.

The middle of the room held a stage on which a spotlight pulsated in different colors, changing the scrawny blonde grinding on the pole from a Smurf to a Martian to a scarlet fever victim then back to blonde. He did not recognize the song whose lyrics amounted to a rhythmic recitation of racially insensitive terms.

He made out small round tables and a few sizable booths arranged in a circle around the stage. He would sit as far from the speakers as possible to keep his insides from quivering while he drank. There were other customers, none of whom made eye contact with him as he crossed the room.

What had @CynthiaGleans said that brought him to this shadowy room? @CynthiaGleans: He thought of her like that, by her handle, had even dreamed of her that way once—not of her scantily clad AVI, just her handle. She'd said, "It can be nice, being touched by a stranger." It had made him wonder if, after months of chatting online, Cynthia was still a stranger to him. And Gabe might have ensouled the fantasy that flew into his thoughts when she'd said the thing about touching a stranger, were she not married. But Gabe was done with married women.

A busty, lime-green corseted waitress took his beer order.

"Where can I get a pack of cigarettes?" he asked.

"There's a vending machine outside the john," she said, pointing to the men's room.

He acquired a pack of Camels. Across the hall from the vending machine, a host of cigars lounged in an unattended, locked glass case. That was how they skirted the smoking ban: the club was also, technically, a tobacco shop—and thus exempt. Having no lighter, he lit a cigarette from the candle burning in a small red cup on his table.

Gabe took a closer look around. A different girl had mounted the stage—a brunette with cartoonish, silicone-plated breasts. She wore a gold dress in a wet-looking fabric that blended almost perfectly with her skin, her face pretty but unsmiling.

He was looking for someone, on Cynthia's suggestion, who looked happy to be there—someone who caught his eye.

The conversation that had brought him there had been less

jocular than those he usually had with Cynthia—more personal than previous exchanges. Cynthia had written that her friend's dog—a "small, smelly, territorial animal"—had persecuted her all week, chasing her around and licking her legs. She found dog saliva disgusting.

Knowing Cynthia seldom left her hometown for more than a day or two, seven days seemed like a long time for her to be away from home. He'd asked why she was staying at a friend's house.

"This friend lives far. I love her. Haven't seen her in over a year. Turns out I know her new poet-husband, too." She paused a minute then added, "She's an ex-lover, Gabe. So is he. I must've needed to hear them finish an English sonnet together at four o'clock this morning. . . You know, to learn my heart still had a spot intact enough to break."

Gabe hadn't known what to say to such a revelation or what color to assign the sad, erotic image it evoked.

Later in the conversation, she'd asked him why he disliked getting haircuts.

"I don't like being touched by strangers," Gabe had told her.

That was when, among other things, she'd said, "I was once mashed against a handsome stranger on a train for three stops. At one point we could have changed positions, but neither of us did.

"I was sad when we came to my stop."

"The exception may prove the rule," Gabe had said, his imagination tumid with the image of Cynthia and the stranger on the train.

She'd continued, "A woman on an airplane once handed me her red-haired baby so she could 'use the bathroom alone for the first time in a year.' It was nice."

"Didn't the baby cry?" Gabe had asked.

"He didn't. He put his fingers all over my face and laughed. I almost died of happiness."

Gabe had never known anyone who'd died of happiness. He struggled, daily, for contentment. Gabe then thought of strangers who had touched him.

"When strangers touch me it's usually a handshake. Mostly I shake hands with poor people who hardly ever shower."

"The people you help in your work?"

"Yes. Sometimes people with track marks on their arms hug me." Occasions, Gabe had thought but not said, on which he struggled to avoid visibly recoiling.

"You've never had a massage?" She'd persisted.

"No." He had almost had a massage. He'd gone with a friend who had a two for one coupon at a spa but left when he learned he'd have to take all his clothes off.

"Hasn't a doctor or nurse ever touched you in a gentle, healing way?"

"No. That's why I only go to the doctor when I think I might die if I don't. I'm much more comfortable," Gabe had said, stroking his German shepherd Trixie between the ears, "being licked by dogs."

The waitress brought his beer. He paid for it and over-tipped her. Gabe ate nothing but canned beans for up to a week between paychecks. Social work paid just enough to keep the lights on, yet he always over-tipped. But tomorrow was payday, and he'd just sold a painting for three-hundred and sixty-five dollars. Gabe smoked with a feeling of satisfaction; he felt rich.

Did anyone look happy to be working there? What kind of woman would find such work fulfilling?

Cynthia had been a stripper in college.

"For the most part, I liked giving lap dances," she'd said. "I'm an affectionate person. If I've ever had a problem touching people, it's been me touching people a little too much. I come from a very affectionate family; I had to learn *not* to touch everyone."

Gabe had wondered what that was like.

"I'm probably not an affectionate person," he'd told her. "But I've never had a lap dance. You're making me feel like maybe I'm missing out on something."

"You should do it!" Cynthia said.

"Maybe."

"You totally should. I want to hear all about it."

A woman dressed as a mermaid smiled at Gabe from several tables over. She had been sitting with a customer, her back to him when he walked in. She had honest-to-God mermaid-type hair. He fantasized for a moment about burying his face in it. And her smile seemed friendly. A handful of other women had met his eyes briefly and smiled, but their smiles had felt, if anything, vaguely hostile. Halfway through his beer, he noticed the other men in the room wore business suits. Him? He only felt rich. In his worn sneakers and button-down flannel shirt, Gabe realized he looked, to these women, like a can of beans.

He extinguished his cigarette.

The mermaid stood up and walked out of the room—the opposite direction of his table—just as another girl sat in the chair next to his.

He was down to his last swig of beer. He could leave.

He didn't leave.

He wondered what the girl would be like. Why she picked his table. If maybe she was an affectionate person. If, as Cynthia suggested, strippers offered comfort to lonely men.

He closed his eyes.

Gabe avoided asking himself if he was lonely. He worked; he painted; he saw his friends; he played with his dog. He sometimes asked himself if he'd be happier with a woman in his life. It was not a simple question for Gabe.

At thirty-four, Gabe lived alone. Most of his friends had married. Some had kids. Thinking about marriage made Gabe's stomach ache. There had been, for three years, a woman—an unhappily married woman—he would have married. And though Gabe liked the idea of kids, he felt it would be stupid—even if by chance a qualified, willing, single woman appeared—to bring children into his penury. Gabe worked with the children of penury. It depressed him.

He hardly noticed he'd closed his eyes—to the smoke, the lights, and his solitude. Gabe was an artist. He collected images and picked out colors and symbols for his paintings. Gabe knew he loved painting more than he could love any woman. Interacting with the person beside him might prove artistically fruitful—but not with his eyes closed.

She hadn't moved.

She smelled strongly of cinnamon. Gabe disliked the smell of cinnamon. He tried to put her scent out of his mind. It wasn't her fault he hated the smell of cinnamon—that it was something the sour grandmother who half-raised him sprinkled on everything including French fries. How could this kindly stripper girl know he associated the smell of cinnamon with his mother abandoning him when he was eleven?

"I'm Diamond," she said, extending a small, white-gloved hand.

"Gabriel." They shook hands. He felt sweaty though the room was cold. He worried he'd sweat onto her glove, so he pulled his hand away quickly.

He'd have to look at her face. He needed another beer. He waved to the waitress, holding up his empty beer bottle, signaling for another.

"I've never seen you here before," Diamond said.

A tarantula he worried he could only wash down with a few more beers stood in his throat.

"Are you having a good night?" Diamond asked.

Politeness compelled Gabe to look at her, so he did.

"I'm shy," he croaked.

"Me, too," she said.

The waitress brought his second beer. He paid.

Diamond looked very young—like she should be on a study date with a boy her age who should have to wait for a few dates before he got to see her naked. She had acne on her forehead and chin that no amount of makeup could conceal. She'd gathered her short, light brown hair in red barrettes on either side of her face. The redness of her lipstick in contrast to the paleness of her skin gave her the air of a naked mime.

She wasn't naked, per se, but her red-and-white-striped dress had a huge cutout in the midsection and only barely covered her elsewhere. Looking at the quantity of breast spilling from the top of her dress made Gabe shift in his seat. It felt wrong to be sexually attracted to someone so much younger.

He drank half the second beer in one gulp.

"How can you be shy and do this job?"

"There's not really a lot of talking," she said.

"What about the other stuff?"

"I'm high."

"Oh."

He gulped down the rest of his beer.

He could leave. He could fake going to the bathroom and

never come back. He thought about the possibility of touching Diamond and stood.

"What happens in a lap dance?" He asked.

"I dance on your lap, put my tits in your face."

He made the mistake of allowing his eyes a dip into her cleavage. It had been a while since he'd seen a woman's naked breasts.

Gabe followed Diamond through a short hallway into an even darker room.

When a new song started, Diamond popped up off the couch, slid her dress down her hips, and straddled him. His arms moved, reflexively, to encircle her waist, but he withdrew at the last second. He did not want to get his fingers broken by whoever broke fingers in this place.

"You can touch me above the waist. If you want," Diamond said, rubbing her large, exquisite breasts against his face.

Gabe sat on his hands. He would not touch her. She could touch him if she chose.

Diamond danced sinuously against him. She felt good in the dark.

"No biting or scratching, though," she added.

"What?"

"No biting or scratching," she repeated.

Who on earth had bitten this girl? Or scratched her? How had he become someone she needed to say that to?

"Would you please put your dress back on," he said, pulling his face as far as he could from her very near breasts.

Diamond burst into tears.

"What's wrong? Did I hurt you?" he asked, panicked both by her tears and by the possibility of encountering this club's knuckle-breaker.

Some of her tears fell on his face before she retreated from his lap.

"What's wrong with my dancing?" she asked, between hiccupping sobs. She sobbed for an entire verse.

"Do people really bite you and scratch you when you dance for them?" Gabe asked.

The tears stopped, but her chest still heaved. Diamond knelt beside him now, carefully avoiding touching him, using the mirror behind the couch to check her makeup.

"Are you buying another dance?" she asked, arms crossed, mouth tight when she stood up. "I can't stay back here if you don't."

He pulled two twenties from his wallet and handed them to her.

She folded them into her garter and stared at him.

Gabe couldn't stand being stared at.

A new song snaked into the room: another unfamiliar song, the lyrics faint.

"I don't turn tricks," she said. "I'll dance for you, but that's it."

"Would you stay dressed and talk to me?"

"It costs the same."

"That's fine."

"Why'd you ask me to get dressed?"

"The biting thing."

"If that's your thing, I know a girl here who likes that—"

"It made me sad."

"That I told you not to bite me? Jesus, you're sick!"

"It made me sad that anyone would hurt you like that. That you thought *I* might hurt you."

"Oh."

The song ended. Diamond stood up, extending her gloved hand by way of goodbye.

Gabe put forty more dollars in her hand.

Diamond sat back down.

"You still haven't told me what made you cry."

Diamond finished her cigarette and dropped it, smoldering, into a nearby ashtray.

"I don't like talking."

Gabe considered leaving. He'd already spent more money than he had planned. He'd had his lap dance—or a fraction of one, anyway. He could tell Cynthia about the plain, temperamental girl with the beautiful breasts who'd wept on him. He could tell it funny, or he could tell it sad. He'd never heard Cynthia's voice, but he liked to imagine her laughter. He'd tell it funny. He could leave now and tell it funny.

He looked again at Diamond.

She started to laugh.

He remembered she was high. Maybe he'd been angsty over her tears when they were nothing more than a drug-induced mood swing?

"I'll buy one more song if you tell me what made you cry. And why you're laughing now."

Her giggles ebbed. She straightened her face—but then laughed again. Louder.

"Do we have a deal?"

"Sure."

"So?"

"What's funny is I've made more money in the last twenty minutes dressed than I normally make in three hours of taking my clothes off—

"I mean, I know I'm not pretty, but you just *paid* me to keep my clothes on."

Gabe had not thought of it that way, but that she could laugh at the irony of it made him like her.

"They'll make fun of me when they find out."

"Who?"

"The other girls."

"Won't they just make fun of me? For being stupid?" Gabe asked.

"You, too, Gabriel. They'll make fun of both of us."

"I'd never bite or scratch you."

Diamond pulled a spaghetti strap off her shoulder and smiled. "We could talk while I dance for you."

Gabe sat back as she straddled him again.

"No one will break my fingers if I put my hands on your waist?"

"No one will break your fingers."

Gabe laid his hands gingerly on her waist.

Acknowledgments

I extend my deepest thanks to:

- My husband, Jim, for propping, co-schlepping, and, in almost all instances, underwriting my dreams.

- My thesis advisor and friend, John Keene, for his mentorship and encouragement.

- The editors of the following publications in which the foregoing stories first appeared:

    - *Queen Mob's Tea House* ("The Pet Store", February 2015)

    - *The Evansville Review* ("Check Engine", Volume XXVII, 2017)

    - *The Acentos Review* ("The Evil Vortex of Doom", May 2015)

    - *Adanna* ("Cream", Issue #8, 2018)

    - *Defunkt Magazine* ("Don't Write About Me, Volume Four)

    - *Glassworks* ("Dreaming of the Netherlands", April 2019); *Fresh Ink* (March 5, 2020)

    - *The London Reader* ("The Baby Monitor", October 2019)

    - *The Bryant Literary Review* ("Death Comes to the Office for Daniel Downer", Volume 19, 2018)

    - *The Northern Virginia Review* ("Mayor Daley at the Superdawg", 2019)

    - *Take a Mind Trip* ("Lap Dance", Scribes Valley Publishing, 2018)

- My writer and non-writer friends and colleagues who have looked over my drafts all these years and never suggested I give up; and,

- You, for spending your finite, irretrievable time reading my collection.

Author Bio

Jennifer Companik holds an M.A. from Northwestern University and is a fiction editor at *TriQuarterly*. The child of South American immigrants, one of her life goals is to travel from Colombia down to Argentina, sampling every region's empanadas along the way—because traveling and empanadas are the meaning of life. Her literary accomplishments include the first prize, *The Ledge*'s 2014 Fiction Awards; a Pushcart Prize nomination from *Border Crossing*; and work appearing in *The Evansville Review, Pop Matters, Glassworks, Another Chicago Magazine,* and *The London Reader*. Her personal accomplishments include every time she makes someone laugh. By reading her book, you are participating in one of her wildest dreams.

9 781734 515893